D1095073

# A Sea of Sorrows

## The Typhus Epidemic Diary of Johanna Leary

BY NORAH MCCLINTOCK

Scholastic Canada Ltd.

*Ireland to Canada East, 1847*

## *April 30, 1847*

When Grandda told me all the stories he had about fairies and pookas and banshees, and about the ancients, such as the great Cuchulain, he said that stories hold a people together. I wonder what he would think if he were still here, for Da says that this great trouble we are in is tearing our people apart. It has sent many to their deaths and now it drives us from our home. That is why I have decided to write down our story. I want to write about what is happening to us and what will happen next.

Tomorrow we leave, and Da says we may never return. He and Ma, Michael, wee Patrick and I are to walk to Dublin, where we will take a steamer to Liverpool in England. He says it is our only hope.

Even in spite of this, Ma is sad to leave. She says, how can we think of making a fresh start in a new land, Canada, when we have to rely on charity to get ourselves there? She says, if anything happens, what will become of us without friends and neighbours close by?

Da reminds her that his bother Liam is in Canada and will surely help us. I barely remember him, I was so small when he left. For myself, I think of Anna

3

going out there last year with her family. I am not afraid. Leaving is like being granted three wishes all at once. When we leave, all the sadness and misery around us will vanish. When we leave, we will go to a place where people eat meat and drink milk every day. When we leave, it will bring the day closer when I will be with Anna again and once more hear Da tease us by calling us AnnaJohanna all in one breath, as if we were one person. I close my ears when Da tells me that I must not get my hopes up. He says that Canada is a big country and that, anyway, many Irish leave Canada to go to America, which is bigger than Ireland. He says that the Irish in America are scattered like the stars across the sky and that any one of them will be hard to find. But how many Anna Riordans can there be? I know I will find her.

### May 1, 1847

I heard Ma crying in the night when everyone else was asleep. She says she would rather go to England, where she is sure a fine carpenter like Da will find work. But Da says things are hard for Irish there and that Canada is a better place. He says it is full of promise. He tries to soothe Ma by reading Uncle Liam's old letters aloud again. Uncle Liam writes that he dines like a king on wheat bread with butter made from the milk of his own cows and on eggs from the chickens he keeps. He eats beef and pork. He makes

4

meat sausage in the autumn that he says smells glorious as it sizzles over the fire. Just thinking about sizzling sausage makes my mouth water, even though I have never eaten it. *Sizzling* is such a fine word. I think that anything that sizzles must taste delicious.

Ma frets that Da has received no letter from Liam in nearly a year. She says something may have happened to him. But Da refuses to worry. He says his brother is probably busy with his animals and his crops. Perhaps he has even married and has a baby to attend to. No matter, he says. A man who has his own land is a man who is always easily found.

### May 3, 1847

I am crouched behind a rock at the side of the road. I do not want Ma to see me. Last year when things got bad, she had to sell or trade everything we had of value — it was the only way to pay our debts and buy food. One by one her precious little store of books left her by her own da, my dear grandda, vanished — all save this little one that I am writing in. I hid it, thinking it worthless to anyone, for many of the pages are used and others are tattered. But if Ma saw me with it, she might become angry.

My feet are sore, my legs ache and my stomach growls like a wild beast. We walked all day yesterday and the day before and have eaten most of the little store of food we brought with us. Da tries to keep our spirits up. He says we are better off than some, and this is true. We passed many wretched-looking people who have nothing at all to eat. One woman wept as she knelt over a man who had collapsed at the side of the road. Some we passed looked like wraiths risen from their shrouds, so hollow were their eyes and so sharply did their bones show through their grey skin. And such tales we have heard! Fifty folk are said to be dying each day in one county. One man swears he has seen coffins with trap doors in the bottom, which allow the coffin maker to sell and use the same coffin over and over. Another tells of two families who died from eating the diseased carcass of a horse.

Da tells us not to listen. He says that if we keep going, we will be on the steamer for Liverpool the day after tomorrow and on our way across the ocean soon after that. I have never been on a steamer before. *Steamer* is another fine word. It makes me think of the little cloud of steam that rises when you break open a potato hot from the fire. I wish I had a potato now, with a little salt and a little milk. Some days I think that all I do is wish.

### May 6, 1847

We left Ireland yesterday and have reached Liverpool at last. *Steamer* is not such a fine word after all. I will be happy if I never have to set foot on another steamer again.

The weather coming across to England was foul. Da says we were lucky to be on deck where people could be sick over the side of the vessel. In the hold, they had to use buckets or the floor. But I did not feel lucky. The wind whipped us the whole way across, and the rain, when it came, drove into my skin like needles of ice. Ma held Patrick close and sang softly to him when she wasn't fretting about how we would manage if the whole journey was as miserable. Da tried to tease her out of her mood. He told her to try for a change to imagine the best instead of the worst. But Ma is not like Da. Ma worries all the time.

### May 7, 1847

From a distance, the stone piers and docks of Liverpool looked quite majestic, but close up they are crowded with people and ships, and the air is filled with shouts and cries, clatters and bangs. You cannot walk more than two paces without being crashed into or having some beggar's hand thrust out before you and a plea made, often by some poor soul from home. The ships in the water jostle each other as roughly as the people on land do. They are not steamers. They are sailing ships. Michael says a steamer would likely run out of coal before it got very far and that we are going very far indeed. Da says that there are steamships that cross the ocean, but they are for rich folk, not for the likes of us.

We are to board our ship tomorrow. Da says this makes us among the fortunate. Some folk arrived in Liverpool a week or more ago and had to spend every penny they had on lodging and food until the ship was ready to sail.

I feel sorry for Da. He tries to keep our spirits up, but Ma smothers his efforts and calls him a dreamer. I remember when she used to say this fondly. There is no fondness in her words now.

### *May 8, 1847*

As we waited to board, I heard someone say that there will be more than three hundred passengers. The ship is large, but still I cannot see how it will fit so many people.

We had to wait for such a long time before boarding that my legs got weary from standing. I sat on the ground and nearly had the life crushed out of me by a great horse of a girl. She was as heavy as a cartload of potatoes when she fell on me, and I know I will be bruised all over. She picked herself up as if she had tripped over a rock and started off again without so much as asking if I was hurt. "Excuse me, I'm sure," I said in a loud voice, but she did not take the hint. Instead, she looked down at me in annoyance and said, "You could have done me an injury sitting in the road like that." She meant it, too! She is the rudest and least handsome girl I ever saw.

I was hot and tired and hungry by the time we filed on board. But instead of being allowed to settle ourselves, we were held at one end of the ship in a great crush. Sailors went down below with long poles that had great spikes at the end. "They are searching for stowaways," Michael whispered. But they must not have found any for they returned empty-handed, and roll call began. When the name Leary was called, Da stepped forward with our tickets, and we were permitted to go below.

### Later

I am glad that our names were called early, for the hold where we are to sleep is as gloomy as a November evening. But because we were among the first to go below, we were able to choose a place close to one of the hatches. Ma keeps looking up at the grey patch of sky above. She doesn't say anything, but I think she is nervous.

The hold seemed large enough when we came down, but it filled quickly. There is hardly any space to walk on the floor (is a floor called a floor in a ship?), and the ceiling is so low that the taller men can barely stand upright.

Our new home, as Da calls it, consists of one berth, which is only a grand name for a bit of plank, like a shelf, set into the side of the ship. The berths are three high and are so close together that you can't even sit up once you've slithered in. I wonder how Anna's family managed. They are seven and have no babies like Patrick, who takes up little space. Perhaps they were allowed two berths. Perhaps Anna got to share with her two sisters and they giggled their way across the ocean.

Ma insisted on a topmost berth. She says that if it collapses — and she seems certain it will — at least we will not be crushed.

Michael counted fifty-two berths altogether, in two rows. Each has five or six people in it. Between the rows there is a narrow aisle for bundles, boxes and chests. Ma says we are stacked and stored like peat. Da says we are as snug as a family of wee swallows in their nest.

The berths to one side of us are taken by the family of the rude girl who nearly trampled me ashore. She is in the top berth, like me. My feet will point at her head the whole way to Canada. I will pretend to dance on it until it aches.

## May 9, 1847

Before we sailed, the captain ordered all the married men above deck. Da said they were told to form a committee and that he was elected head of it. The committee's job is to keep watch during the night to make sure there are no irregularities, to alert the captain if anyone falls ill, and to secure the hatches if there is a storm.

Ma looked frightened when he mentioned the word *storm*. I asked what irregularities the committee is to watch for. Da said, with a wink, that it must make sure all the young men and young women are where they are supposed to be and not where they should not be. Ma told him to hush.

Da also said that we must air our bedding and dry-scrub our berths twice a week. No one is allowed to smoke or light a fire below deck.

Finally, he said that we would receive one week's rations at a time and that each family must take turns sending someone above to cook meals. The rations are mostly oatmeal. On some days we will get ship's biscuit. Da does not know what the biscuit tastes like.

There are two fireplaces on the deck for cooking. I climbed the ladder to peek at them. They are big wooden boxes lined with bricks, and they have metal grates set on them. Da says they will be lit at seven every morning, if the weather is fine enough, and put out at sunset. I do not know what we are supposed to do when the weather is not fine. Some of the older boys were asked to keep the deck clean and the cistern filled with water. Michael raised his hand to volunteer. The great ugly girl from the next berth started to raise her hand as well. Her da grabbed hold of it and jerked it down. He told her to get her head out of the clouds.

Patrick was fussing, so Ma sent me to cook the oatmeal. I was afraid to go. What if I fell overboard? What if I ruined the meal? Mrs. Keenan, the rude girl's mother, offered to help me. She is very nice. I don't know how she could have raised such an unpleasant daughter.

The fireplace wasn't as hard to cook on as I feared. I didn't burn the oatmeal. The rude girl gobbled her food like a pig. Mrs. Keenan did not scold her.

### May 10, 1847

I am not afraid to go up on the deck anymore. In fact, I was glad to go up today so that I could breathe some fresh air. Now that the ship is underway, many people are sick. There is so much groaning and vomiting below. I heard the captain tell Da that those new to the sea often take ill. He said it always reminds him of the psalm about going down to the sea in ships. He quoted the verse: "They reel to and fro and stagger like a drunken man and are at their wit's end."

Michael is sick. So is Ma. Da looks pale but says he is fine. I do not think I believe him. I am not bothered at all.

### May 11, 1847

Too queasy to write much. Michael says it serves me right for being prideful about not getting ill in the first place.

### May 12, 1847

Stomach turning every which way. Still too queasy to write.

### May 13, 1847

I hate ships as much as I hate steamers.

### May 14, 1847

I woke up this morning feeling better. When I took out my book to write, Ma caught me at it. I thought she would be angry, but she was not. She asked me what I was doing with it. When I told her, all she said was that she hoped it would not turn out to be a book of sorrows. She left Patrick with me and went above to cook. It took her an eternity, but she returned with an extra-large portion of oatmeal. She said we can afford it as we have barely touched the week's rations.

I was surprised how ravenous I was. I ate until I was stuffed. I wonder if Uncle Liam does the same every day — only with sausage instead of oatmeal.

### May 15, 1847

Michael has been grinning like a fool all day but won't tell me why. He says it's a secret. He can be so annoying.

I went above with Ma to cook oatmeal cakes.

There are always women crowded near the fireplaces. Some of them cook. Some of them wait impatiently to cook. All of them chatter and gossip. We saw three sailors sitting in a row with their legs straight out in front of them, mending sails. Mrs. Keenan said that she wished Mr. Keenan would learn to mend for it would make her work lighter.

There is nothing around us but water. It is frightening to think what would become of us if the ship were to strike something and sink. Who would save us?

I haven't seen the rude girl in days, and just as well.

### May 16, 1847

After services on the deck this morning, I discovered Michael's secret. He is furious with me. I saw him creep to the farthest end of the hold and tuck himself behind a pile of trunks and boxes secured with rope. I crept close and listened. The secret is this: The rude Keenan girl is a boy! His name is Connor and he is wanted by the authorities. Although he is scarcely older than Michael, he and a band he is with threatened and robbed some of the landlords. His temper flared when I said that stealing is a sin.

"If that is so, then why are the landlords and the merchants not charged for stealing the bounty of Ireland and selling it abroad while the people of Ireland starve to death?" he demanded. And he went on and on about that coroner in County Waterford saying that so many deaths there were caused by "the negligence of the government" in not providing food to the people.

Michael agreed with him immediately, saying that while the potatoes rot and common folk starve, the landlords have been selling oats, wheat, barley, beef and pork abroad. I did not have to ask where he had heard this, for Connor nodded with every word. Nor could I dispute what he said, though the heartlessness of the landlords does not excuse the sin of robbery. But I was not in a mood to argue about what was right and what was wrong, especially when the two of them would have countered every word. Instead, I looked at Connor.

"I have heard that a person's opinions may break his nose or even cut his throat," I said. "But never have I heard of a person's mouth turning him into a girl, although in your case it clearly has. And a clumsy one at that."

"Pay no attention to my baby sister," Michael said.

I hate when he calls me that, as if I'm a mere child.

"I'm no baby," I said. "I'm thirteen. And you're only a year older than I, Michael Leary."

"A year and a half," Michael sniffed, as if that made all the difference.

Connor laughed and said he had never met a baby with such a sharp tongue, but he didn't seem at all put out. He said that his ma was so afraid he would be arrested and hanged that she dressed him as a girl and claimed he was her daughter, but that no matter how hard he tried, he could never master a girl's ways.

### May 19, 1847

It has been days since I have written, for no sooner had I left Michael and Connor above deck than Da and Mr. Sullivan came down to announce that a storm was coming. That set Mrs. Tattersall to wailing. Mr. Tattersall said that she is deathly afraid of the sea. She dreamt while they waited at Liverpool that she and her babies fell into the ocean and were swallowed up by waves, and that she had clawed her way through the cold water to try to catch them as they dropped like stones into the bottomless sea. She woke up screaming.

Da said we mustn't panic, although I noticed that he fingered his little tin St. Joseph medal, which he always does when he's whispering a prayer. (It is a poor thing, dented in one side. St. Joseph himself is worn almost smooth from Da's rubbing him with his thumb, but it has hung around Da's neck for as long as I can remember.) He said the captain would shut the hatches to keep the water from coming in. That set another woman to wailing, and her terror made some of the wee 'uns cry. Da went to her and told her calmly but firmly she mustn't carry on so, as it set a poor example for the children. The woman clamped her mouth shut as if God had reached down and pinched it closed. She looked up at Da, her face as white as lace, her eyes as black as coal, and nodded.

The storm came upon us like an army of banshees. The wind howled as it tore at the vessel. The hatches were closed, and all went dark. We were not allowed to have even one candle for fear of fire. With the dark came silence from every man, woman and child, and that seemed to encourage the wind, whose howls became battle cries as it first rocked and then shook the vessel.

At first everyone made a grand effort. Somewhere a woman sang a soft lullaby to a whimpering baby. I heard Ma murmuring prayers beside me. I whispered one myself, for even though I was determined to be as brave as Da, the truth was that I was in terror. What if the ship did not hold? What if it were overwhelmed by waves? There was no land in sight and no one to come to our rescue.

After a long time of being tossed about and shrieked at by the wind, I heard a crash, like a shelf full of crockery smashing onto a flagstone floor.

Then I heard screaming. Had a wave broken through the side of the ship? Had falling boxes crushed someone? It was impossible to tell in the dark.

Over the wailing of passengers and the wind, I heard Da call for help. Chests and boxes had cascaded to the floor of the hold and had to be secured so that they did not smash or, worse, damage the hull. Michael scrambled from our berth to lend his hand to the task.

I lay in my place, curled like a frightened lamb and clutching the edge of the plank so as not to be tossed below.

How the storm went on. There was no way of knowing the true passage of time for we could not see the sun or the moon or the stars. There was only darkness quickly followed by the stench of sick and waste as buckets toppled and the awful shaking and shuddering roiled our stomachs.

I thought of Noah and the great flood he had endured with his wee ark packed tight with all the creatures of the world. Did he feel as sick and frightened as I did? Or did his faith give him strength?

The hold grew so rank with sick and foul air that someone — I do not know who — proposed to break open the hatch to get some air. Others took up the cry, and Da had to argue mightily to get them to see that this would put the ship in danger of foundering.

At long last the storm abated. I had fallen asleep

and was woken by the calm and silence. The hatch had been opened, and a shaft of moonlight falling into the foul hold illuminated a standing figure. 'Twas Da, his head was uplifted, and his eyes were closed. I cannot be sure, but I think he was giving thanks.

## *May 20, 1847*

There has been much cleanup and repair to do, but everyone is in good spirits. The captain told Da that the storm was as bad as any he has ever seen, and it must be a good omen that no one was lost in it. Some men, Da among them, have been helping the crew mend the rigging and the masts. All the women and the children who are able have been cleaning below. Many were sick during the storm, and none of the waste could be emptied. Most of it slopped onto the floor, which we scrubbed now as best as our arms and backs would allow. We washed and aired the bedding and disposed of the waste.

Connor had to stay below and clean even though he would rather go above. Most of the passengers know by now that he is a boy. But there are none who will betray him. When he goes above, which is rarely, he covers his head with a shawl and stays behind his mother like a great shy hulk of a girl.

## May 21, 1847

The captain himself came to inspect the hold. It is whispered that fear of ship's fever fills his mind. Many are grumbling that the absence of illness is a miracle, so poor is the food that the shipping company has provided. And to think that some of these grumblers were starving little more than a fortnight ago!

## May 22, 1847

This morning as I made my way above deck to cook the breakfast, I heard Mrs. Tattersall whisper to Ma that Mr. Tattersall is feeling poorly. He lay awake all night with aches in his arms and legs. Ma says she must tell the captain, for he has a medicine chest and may be able to help. Mrs. Tattersall agreed even though Mr. Tattersall said it was nothing. The captain came and dosed Mr. Tattersall with a purgative. He remained in his berth all day.

## May 23, 1847

Mr. Tattersall was up and about this morning and came to services on deck. His face was pale, but he whistled a fine tune for his babies while Mrs. Tattersall was above deck making stirabout. But by midday, he was back in his berth, trembling like a nestling in a gale. Soon he was fevered and moaning.

The captain came again with his medicine. When he turned to climb above, he motioned for Da to follow him. Da returned, his face sombre as a judge's, but he forced a smile when Ma asked him if anything was amiss. She did not press the matter, but I could not stop wondering what the captain had said to him.

### May 24, 1847

Mr. Tattersall is in a stupor. He lies motionless in his berth, barely drawing breath and mewling like an infant. Mrs. Tattersall is beside herself.

Mrs. Donnell has aches and fever. So do some of the other passengers.

### May 27, 1847

I have been so busy the past few days. Ma has been helping with all the little Tattersalls so that Mrs. Tattersall could nurse Mr. Tattersall. I am left in charge of Patrick, who does nothing but fuss.

### May 28, 1847

Sad news. Mr. Tattersall has died. His passing was discovered this morning when Mrs. Tattersall woke to find him cold beside her. How she wailed. The little Tattersalls did likewise. Ma did her best to calm them all while Da went above to tell the captain, who was down below in a trice with two crewmen to take Mr. Tattersall aloft. The captain and Da went through the hold and spoke to each family. When the captain left, Da looked troubled.

Within the hour, the crewmen had sown Mr. Tattersall into a shroud and weighted the shroud with a stone. The captain read a passage from the Scriptures, and Mr. Tattersall was laid to his rest in the ocean while Mrs. Tattersall wept. Her terrible dream had come true after all, except that it is Mr. Tattersall, not her babies, who has sunk below the waves.

### May 30, 1847

Two more passengers have been sent to their rest in the sea. While we stood above deck after the service, someone spotted a shark. Someone else muttered about being flung into the brine like rotten sheep into a pit.

More people are ill.

### June 1, 1847

Mr. Keenan, Connor's da, is ill with the fever. So is Connor's sister Colleen. Mrs. Keenan is nursing them as best she can. Connor has been charged with looking after his brothers: Kerry, Kevin and wee Daniel. Michael and I are helping him. I have been telling them stories about what awaits us in Canada. I have Uncle Liam and his letters to thank for that. Kevin keeps asking me to describe a moose to him.

I do the best I can: Uncle Liam says a moose is taller than a man, with antlers that are broader than the full span of a grown man's arms. He says one moose will feed a family for the whole winter.

Kerry wants to know about bears and wolves and other wild things with claws and fangs. He boasts that he will learn to hunt when he gets to Canada and that no wild beast will be safe when he is about. Daniel, who is only three, buries his head in Connor's chest every time Kerry growls like a bear.

Ma is worried about Patrick, who has been whining and crying all day. Da says it is most likely a tooth coming in, but Ma refuses to believe this. She is terrified that he will get the fever.

### June 3, 1847

Eileen Cairns, eight, and Thomas Kelleher, ten, died during the night. Their mothers wept bitterly. Mrs. Kelleher would not relinquish her grip on Thomas. Da had to get Ma and some of the other women to hold her so that Thomas could be taken above for burial. When his body was finally put into the ocean, Mrs. Kelleher rushed to the side of the ship to follow him. It was only the quick action of the first mate that saved her. He grabbed at her skirts and let out a shout. Two sailors rushed to his aid, but even so the three of them had a struggle on their hands to stop her from plunging into the deep.

Mr. Kelleher finally grasped her around the waist and clung tightly to her. He was weeping.

"The poor man," Da said, shaking his head. Ma held Patrick tightly. I heard her whisper to Da that he has lost his appetite and feels hot to the touch.

Later, Connor told me that he heard Mr. Kelleher say that he was sorry he ever left Ireland. He said it would have been better if Thomas had died at home where he could be buried in the ground with a priest to say words over him, instead of being tossed into the ocean like so much refuse.

Michael argued that if the Kellehers had stayed home, they would likely be dead from starvation by now. "At least we have food on the ship, however poor it is," he said.

Connor agreed. But he also said that when you are buried in the ocean, it is as good as being forgotten. Your family can never visit you where you lie or point out your resting place to those who come after you. He shuddered when he said it. Michael teased that a spirit must have walked over his grave. I jabbed him hard with my elbow. Too many are ill for such a ghoulish joke.

### June 5, 1847

Connor says that Colleen is covered from head to toe with blotches and that his da sleeps fitfully. Kevin and Kerry are also feeling poorly. Mrs. Keenan is wearing herself out tending to them all.

Patrick was fretful all day when he wasn't sleeping. Ma tends to him constantly, cooling his brow with water and trying to get him to drink a little.

Last night as I lay wedged between Ma and Michael, I had an awful worry. What if there was a fever on Anna's ship? What if she had fallen ill? What if . . .

I don't even want to write the words. I decided to say a special prayer for her every night.

Connor and Michael and I seem to have become the keepers of the children. We gather them above deck where the air is fresh and good, and do our best to amuse them so that their mothers can tend to their chores and, increasingly, their patients. I have gone through every tale, riddle and song that I know and all the games that may be played in a small space.

### June 8, 1847

I have been too busy to write. Connor's father died two days ago. Colleen followed him. Kevin is poorly. Mrs. Keenan is beside herself with grief. On top of that, our Patrick is worse. Ma will not relinquish him for even one moment, even though Da offers to take him so that she can rest. She cradles him and sings to him and tries to get him to swallow a little food to keep up his strength.

To make matters worse, a storm started to blow

just as the service was being read for the dead — four in all, including Connor's da and sister. Immediately afterward, the hatches were battened again. For two long days and nights, the wind howled and the ocean tossed our ship as if it were no more than a twig on the waters. Mrs. Kelleher wailed that the storm was brought on by the restless dead, lashing out in anger because they were not laid to rest in consecrated ground. She moaned as loud as the gale all night. Then she fell silent. I heard Mr. Kelleher tell Ma that she is feverish.

I wish this voyage would end. I wish we were in Canada. Uncle Liam says the air is clean and clear there. He says there are trees for as far as a man can walk in a week, maybe even farther, and that the forests are filled with the music of birds, some of which he had never seen in Ireland.

### June 9, 1847

Our Patrick is gone.

He died so quietly, poor wee thing. Ma is inconsolable. She blames herself. "If I had listened to you," she says over and over to Da. "If only we had left last year, when Liam sent money to pay for decent passage. If only we had not been reduced to this."

Da says "if only" is easy to say but difficult to predict. He tells Ma that no one could have foretold how bad things would become. But Ma doesn't seem to hear him. Over and over again she mumbles to herself, "If only . . . if only."

Da had to coax Patrick from her arms. He held Ma all through the funeral. I think he was remembering Mrs. Kelleher.

### June 10, 1847

I never noticed how much space Patrick took up in our lives. He was such a small thing and so sweet and quick to smile. But now that he is gone, our berth seems so quiet and empty, and Ma does not seem to know what to do with herself. Da comforts her, but he has a faraway look in his eyes, and I imagine he is remembering Patrick.

### June 11, 1847

Mrs. Kelleher has died, and I am worried about Ma. She did not get out of the berth today. She refused to eat the porridge I brought her. I hope she does not fall ill. I don't think I could bear it if anything happened to her or if we had to leave her in the sea.

The weather seems to have caught the mood of the ship. It has been raining since last night. Da organized a few men to catch some of the soft rainwater to drink, as the ship's water smells and tastes foul. As well, people continue to complain about the food. The biscuit has so much horse bran in it that it is hard to digest and is making people ill. I dream about the potatoes Ma used to pull from the fire. So soft and fluffy they were, and so delicious with a little milk and a pinch of salt — my heart aches for home when times were good.

### June 12, 1847

Ma is up and about today. She does not speak, but goes silently about her chores. Annie Malone in the berth below us shivers under her shawl despite the sweltering heat in the hold.

### June 13, 1847

Ma stayed in the berth all day with her face to the wall and did not even attend services. Da lay beside her and held her hand. He says her heart is broken because of Patrick. He says she loves Michael and me both, but that she has weathered the passing of four babes now and that she loved each one of them too. He says the hardest thing for a mother is to lose a babe.

Word came below late in the day that one of the sailors had died of the fever and was sent into the sea. Michael says that sailors are accustomed to such fates.

## June 14, 1847

Three more have died, Kevin Keenan among them. Still more are ill.

## June 15, 1847

Da shook Michael and me awake this morning. I sat up with such a start that I banged my head on the ceiling. My thoughts went to Ma, and I touched her hand. It was warm and she stirred.

"Come above," Da said.

Michael and I climbed the ladder after him. He pointed to something in the distance.

"Canada?" Michael asked, seeming dazed to see land at last.

"That is called Cape Breton," Da said, "from when the French were here. We have come far, and the journey has been hard. But it is almost done."

We stood beside Da for a long time. We passed another island, which the captain called St. Paul Island. There was a lighthouse on it. Da said that means there is a lighthouse keeper as well. But if there is anyone else living on the island, they stayed well hidden.

Later we passed into the Gulf of St. Lawrence, where we saw whales! There were five of them, and massive they were.

## June 16, 1847

The ship is moving so slowly that a man ashore could surely make faster progress. But we are in Canada, and from the ship can see hills and woods and neat little farmhouses at the river's edge.

## June 17, 1847

I was on deck again admiring the billowy clouds above, the rich green of the fields and forests, and the deep blue of the water when I had a terrible fright. I looked down and saw a body floating in the water. A terror went through me for it had no shroud, and I thought of all those we had buried at sea. I whispered a prayer and turned away, but I think the sight will haunt me.

## June 18, 1847

We have reached Quebec City, which is on the north shore of the St. Lawrence River, and the captain has ordered a general cleanup. He says that the government of Canada will send an inspector to the ship. Because we have had the fever on board, those who are unwell will be sent to a hospital on the island called Grosse Isle, which lies just off Quebec. Those who are well will be quarantined. The captain could not say how long the quarantine will last.

For my part, I cannot wait to get off this ship. We

are fewer than when we boarded, but Da says that those of us who are still standing must carry on.

## *June 21, 1847*

Da's da always used to say, "Be careful what you wish for." I used to think it an odd thing to say. After all, if it is something your heart yearns for, what is there to be careful of? Now I know. We spent two days wishing for the doctor to come and inspect us, and all the while I was impatient to get off the ship. But when he arrived, things did not turn out as I had imagined.

The captain had us all line up in rows. The doctor was a tall dour man who never once allowed himself to smile. I saw his head over top of the people in front of me. He paused before he had gone five paces, and a wail went up. I couldn't see what had happened, but Michael soon had it whispered to him from Connor, who was ahead of him. A woman was ordered to the hospital, but her children who are declared healthy may not go with her. As her husband was buried at sea, the children have no one to look after them, and she worries what will become of them. In the end, Da did what he could to assure her that they would be cared for.

Before the doctor passed the end of the first row, two more were plucked from our ranks to be sent to the hospital. One was a single man who had no one to protest his going. Another was a child whose mother was determined to go with him. The doctor was just as determined that she would not.

By the time the inspector reached our bedraggled little row, fully one third of the passengers in front of us had been taken aside for transport to the hospital. I tried to hold myself stiff so as not to betray any trembling, but I breathed such a huge sigh of relief when the doctor passed me by that he turned to look at me again. His eyes were small and muddy behind his spectacles, and he stared so hard at me that I thought he was giving me the evil eye. Finally he turned and moved on to Michael, who was also passed, and then to Ma. As he peered at her I noticed, as if for the first time, how thin and frail she was in contrast to the sturdy doctor. I saw patches of pink on her cheeks. The doctor signalled her to step aside. She did not move.

The doctor repeated his words sharply this time, as if Ma was wasting his time by not obeying him immediately. Still Ma did not move. The doctor turned to the captain for help. The captain turned to Da. The two had come to respect each other. Da had remarked more than once on the captain's skill and his concern for his passengers, which, Da said, was not shown by every sea captain. The captain, for his part, always addressed Da as Mr. Leary and never condescended to him. Whenever there was a problem with the passengers, he sent for Da and listened when Da advised him on how to proceed. So when I saw a look in the captain's eyes that seemed to me to be one of deep concern for Da, I felt a tremble go through me.

Da and the captain looked at each other for what seemed like ages. Then Da said, "Come, Eileen," and helped Ma from the ranks. He spoke into her ear and kissed her and held her for a moment before she was led away.

Mrs. Keenan was among those who were to be taken away. The doctor looked long and hard at Connor, his head covered as usual with his shawl. I was afraid he would be sent away too. Michael was afraid he would be discovered. Connor swears the doctor knew him for a boy, but for some reason let him be. Connor is grateful. There is no one else to look after Kerry and Daniel.

### June 22, 1847

I was so worried about Ma and afraid of what might happen to her that I cried until Michael lost patience and told me I must be strong. He says they have taken Ma to the hospital on Grosse Isle (it means "large island" in French), and that there are nurses and doctors there to care for the ill. For his part, Michael has done nothing but grumble. He had thought that once the ill were removed from the ship, the rest of us would be free to go ashore. But we are not. We must stay on board for six more days so that the authorities can be sure that no one else falls ill.

### June 23, 1847

Rumours are flying from passenger to passenger. Some say that there are two dozen ships and more waiting for medical inspection and to send their ill ashore. Some say they will keep us on the ship for weeks. Some say we will be ashore sooner. On our ship, those who are well have divided into two groups. First there are those who have family members in the hospital. Many of these, especially the women, are in despair that they will never see their loved ones again. Then there are those who have no loved ones in hospital and who deem themselves healthy. They demand to be put ashore. If that cannot happen, then they demand food and fresh water.

This is proving difficult to obtain. The captain says it is because there are so many ships and so many ill. As well, the people who live in Quebec want little to do with those of us on ships. They see us as bringing disease to their towns. Michael says that he heard the captain tell one of the mates that the newspapers are filled with editorials about the Irish lords shovelling their garbage into Canada. Meanwhile, people continue to fall ill, which causes more unrest and panic.

Several of the men went to the captain and angrily demanded to know if the government of Quebec planned to keep us anchored in the St. Lawrence River until we all die of either ship's fever or starvation and thirst. No one is happy.

I think about Ma all the time and pray she will get well.

## June 24, 1847

Nine more passengers have fallen ill and are being taken ashore. Everyone is in poor spirits, especially as news has come back to us that three children, two women and two men from the ship have died in hospital. Ma is not among them, for which I am thankful. But there is some confusion about the other names and so Connor is worried. He does not know if his ma is alive or dead.

## June 25, 1847

Another rumour is flying about. Because there are so many ships waiting in the river, we will be allowed to leave a few days early and will be transported to Montreal. Many people are excited to hear this, but I am not. We have had no news about Ma. The captain has told Da he will do his best to find out how she is, but he warns that this may not be easy. There are more than one thousand ill on the island, and the nurses and doctors are worked to the bone.

## *June 26, 1847*

I woke in the night to whispering. It was Michael. I did not see who he was whispering to, but 'twas easy enough to guess because a moment later wee Daniel, sound asleep, was handed into our berth and settled next to me. Da, beside me, did not stir. Michael slipped into the Keenan berth, saying that he was going to keep an eye on Kerry. I began to ask why Connor wasn't watching both of his brothers, but Michael silenced me. I didn't find out until hours later what had happened.

I tried my best to stay awake but dozed off. When next I opened my eyes, Michael was lifting Daniel down into Connor's arms. Connor was soaking wet. He didn't say a word. Only later, at breakfast, did Michael tell me that Ma was still alive, but that Connor said she was so feverish that she was not in her right mind. He glanced up at our berth where Da was still sleeping. "I do not think you should tell Da."

"How does Connor — ?" I began before remembering him dripping on the floor of the hold.

Connor had gone ashore to look for his ma. While he was there, he looked for ours as well. I asked Michael how Mrs. Keenan was. The sombre look in my face told me that she had passed.

"But what are we going to do?" I asked. "We can't leave without Ma."

"Da will talk to the captain," Michael said. "There

must be some way we can find her if she gets well."

"You mean *when* she gets well," I said sharply.

Michael did not correct himself. He did not say another word.

### June 28, 1847

Kerry Keenan has been taken ashore to the hospital. Or, rather, I should say that he was wrenched from Connor's arms, for Connor did not want to let him go, saying that he would die in that hospital for certain.

"He will die if he is not attended to," the captain said. "And others who are healthy will fall ill. You will fall ill."

In the end, four of the captain's men had to hold Connor, who fought like a wild thing to get free, while Kerry was taken from the ship. At first they seemed astonished to see so much fight in a girl. Then one cried out in dismay, "She's a lad, not a lass." Still Connor punched and kicked until finally one of the mates hit him from behind and he crumpled onto the deck of the ship. The captain has ordered him locked up until we leave the ship tomorrow.

Da spoke to the captain, who agreed not to have Connor arrested and handed over to the authorities, even though his girl's disguise clearly marked him as wanted. He told Da that he does this only out of pity for so many losses in Connor's family and only on the condition that Connor give no more trouble.

Michael and I are minding Daniel.

### July 3, 1847

I am writing this in Montreal, and my heart still aches with a greater sadness than I have ever known.

I tried to get it down before, but I wasn't able to. I will try again now.

When we were finally allowed off the ship three days ago, it was to board a steamer for Montreal, which is said to be two days' journey upstream. Connor, dressed now in boys' clothes, was grateful for what the captain had done, and thanked him before he left the ship. But when we set down on Grosse Isle and the first mate denied him permission to visit Kerry in the hospital, Connor tried to break free again.

What a commotion that caused! I cannot say what came over me, but while everyone else was distracted by Connor, I fled to the hospital myself. I can no more imagine leaving Ma than Connor can imagine leaving Kerry, and I wanted to tell her that we will find her again when she is well and strong.

I slowed as I approached the first rough building, which was ringed with tents. Never have I seen so many people so ill and so crowded together. I stood with my mouth agape as I gazed at the rows of wretched patients lying cramped and filthy in beds.

More than once I saw two poor souls side by side on the same cot. Many were mere skin and bone. Some moaned in agony or for release. I decided that I must be in the shed for the sickest patients for whom there is no hope. Thank goodness I did not see Ma among them.

I turned to leave when I heard a weak cry for water. I am ashamed to say that I could not tell whether the person crying out was a man or a woman, so dirty was the face, so matted the hair, and so wasted the figure. I looked about, but saw no nurse or doctor or indeed anyone who might answer the cry. But I saw a barrel and made for it. A dipper hung from its side. I plunged it into the water and carried it to the person who had cried out. He — when I got close enough, I saw from the fuzz on his face that it was a young man — could not raise his head to drink. I had to slide my hand beneath him to help raise him up. And, oh, the stench from the mouldering straw beneath him! I know it is wrong for me to say this, but he smelled of death. As he gulped at the water, others around him cried out. They were thirsty too. I went back and forth to the barrel of water to help as many as I could. But then I began to worry that the steamer would sail without me, carrying Da and Michael away to Montreal where I would never find them. So I left those poor people crying out and ran to another shed in search of Ma.

When I first saw her, my heart soared. Her eyes were open so I smiled and waved. She did not smile back or lift a hand to wave.

As I ran to her, I saw that she was lying on the ground with not even a sheet under her. I fell to my knees in the muck beside her. Her eyes stared up at the plank ceiling. My fingers trembled as I reached to touch her face. It felt cold to my fingertips. I let out a howl. Just then, two hands seized me from behind and pulled me to my feet.

It was Michael. "Johanna, you must come," he said. "The ship is leaving."

Then his eyes went to the sad figure on the ground before me, and a gasp escaped his lips. He reached out and touched Ma's face. For a moment he seemed unable to move, just stared at her. Then with a trembling hand he closed her eyes.

"Da is waiting," he managed to say, pulling me away.

I was blinded by tears and stumbled as he pulled me along like a wagon. When we reached the ship I could not make myself look at Da. I left it to Michael to tell him what we had seen.

Poor Da. Tears sprang to his eyes when he heard Michael's news, and his fingers went to the St. Joseph medal around his neck as he mouthed a prayer for Ma. He closed his eyes and did not speak for a few minutes. I don't know for certain what was in his mind, but his stillness made he think that he was remembering Ma the way she was when times were good, or perhaps when they had first courted. He had often boasted that she was the prettiest girl he had ever met and how clever he had been to steal her heart. When he finally opened his eyes again, he put one arm around me and the other around Michael and held us close. We were all he had now.

We were all each of us had.

The journey up the river took two long days and nights, with all of us jammed together on the deck of a steamship like so many pieces of wood. There was so little room that anyone who sat was in great danger of being trampled — not that I cared. All I could think about was Ma dying alone in that terrible place. Da and Michael must have been thinking the same thing, for they never spoke. We clung to each other, while Connor cradled Daniel.

One whole day it rained, drenching us to our skins. All that night we shivered. Despite the discomfort, I fell asleep on my feet and did not wake until someone jostled me. It was a crew member who, with one of his mates, was removing a passenger who had died in the night.

When at last we arrived at our destination, we pressed forward to get off the ship. No sooner had we set foot on land than Da collapsed. Michael bent to him and laid a hand on his forehead. His face was grim when he looked up at me. "He is fevered," he said.

Da was taken from us. A man said he would be at the immigrant sheds, where there was a hospital. Michael, Connor, Daniel and I were herded to another area where nuns and other women were waiting to gather the orphaned children. One of the women scooped up Daniel. Connor was on her in an instant, yelling as he pulled his brother away. Two men appeared and grabbed Connor. I tried to hear what was happening, but someone was talking to me, asking if I had parents yet alive. It was a nun. She said if I would come with her, she would see me washed and dressed and fed. I turned to Michael.

"Go," he said. "They will look after you. I'll see to Connor, and then I will find you."

A man wrestled Daniel from Connor and handed him to the same sister who had approached me. He was about to call for help to restrain Connor. But when I promised Connor that I would take care of Daniel, he left off his struggle.

"I'll come and get you," Connor promised his brother.

The sisters took us girls and small boys to a large house where they fed and bathed us and gave us clean clothes to wear. All the girls are to sleep in one large room. The boys are to sleep in another. Everyone is quiet. Now that we are clean and clothed, I can see how hollow-eyed and pale everyone else is. I wonder if I look so deathly.

### July 4, 1847

Only a few of the sisters speak English. The sister in charge of the house, Sister Marie-France, told us that the archbishop has called on parishioners to open their homes and their hearts to Irish orphans. She says we must not worry, for she is sure of a good response. The people of Montreal can see with their own eyes how many orphans are in need of a home and a good Catholic upbringing. I feel glad for the little ones who are truly on their own. But what will become of me? I am not an orphan.

### July 7, 1847

Disaster has struck! A family has taken Daniel for their own. It was only by chance that I happened to find out. I was sweeping the upstairs hall (we have all been given chores) when I heard a child cry. I looked down and saw that it was Daniel. A woman had his hand, but he was tugging to get away from her. He almost managed. But a man who was with the woman scooped him up into his arms. I called for them to stop. Daniel, for his part, was kicking against the man as hard as he could, but he is so small and weak that he was no more threatening than a squirming kitten.

I ran for the stairs. In my haste, I collided with a nun who appeared as if from nowhere, carrying a huge pile of fresh linen. I apologized as I skirted around her, but she grabbed my wrist and pressed her face close to mine. "You must pick up the linen," she said sharply. I promised that I would, but said I had something important to do first. She would not let me go. Finally, I scooped up all the linen in a great armful and thrust it at her, almost bowling her over. Then I raced down the stairs, but too late. Too late. Daniel had been loaded into a wagon and was disappearing around a distant corner.

I could not believe my eyes! I promised to care for him, and now he is gone. I have let Connor down and feel terrible because of it. I will ask Sister Marie-France who has taken Daniel, so that Connor can get him back.

### July 10, 1847

Someone has offered to take me in, but I have refused. My da is alive. Michael is alive. Uncle Liam awaits news of us and we of him. I am not an orphan. Sister Marie-France says that she will write to Uncle Liam, but she warns that she will not be able to keep me forever. She was very kind when she said it, and for that I am grateful.

## July 12, 1847

I have asked many times for permission to visit the hospital sheds, but Sister Marie-France denies me. So today I did what my head tells me was wrong but that my heart insists was right. I slipped away while I was supposed to have been at chores.

I had no idea how to get to the sheds, so I asked a man selling fruit on the street. He gave me a sharp look but pointed out the direction I should take. I promptly lost my way in the bustling city and was forced to stop a gentleman in the street to ask again for directions. He turned up his nose at me and walked away without a word. In the end, it was a lad no older than myself who told me the route. He also said that when I got close enough, I had only to follow the masses. When I asked what masses, he shook his head and told me that I would see.

I repeated his directions to myself as I walked so that I would not forget them. It was not long before I saw a crowd of people headed in the same direction. I hurried to catch up with them and was astonished to find out that although they appeared to be going to the same place I was, they were not Irish. I soon discovered that they had come to gawk and to chatter idly about my poor countrymen. A brother from one of the orders tried to shoo them off, but they persisted. I went round the farthest edges of the crowd and slipped into a shed. Oh, what a sight!

Along the outer walls of the shed were row upon row of rough-made beds, each containing two souls. In the middle, more rough beds had been scattered and, between them, heaps of straw on the floor, with people lying atop them. I stopped before I had gone two paces and held my hand to my nose, so foul was the stench. A glance at the poor wretches closest to me showed me that they lay in their own waste. Tears filled my eyes as I walked up one row, peering into hollowed eyes and waxen faces, praying that I would find no one I knew. I was shocked and saddened to see that some lay dead and had not yet been removed from their bedmates who, in all truth, seemed indifferent. One young lad called out for food. Another wanted water. But nowhere in their midst did I find Da.

That, at least, was a small blessing.

One of the sisters noticed my absence and reported it to Sister Marie-France. She was kind but stern when she told me I must not wander off on my own. I did not tell her where I had gone.

### July 13, 1847

This morning while I was outside hanging clothes with another girl, I heard my name. When I turned I could scarcely believe my eyes, for there was Michael, clean-scrubbed and jumping down from a wagon driven by an older man. I ran to him and threw myself at him, never minding the fence that stood as high as my waist between us. He hugged me close for a moment and then held me at arm's length and laughed as he said he could not remember when he had seen me so well-dressed. I laughed, for I was wearing a patched and faded dress that had been donated to the sisters and cut down to fit me. I asked if he'd had word from Da, but he had not, although he said that he'd tried, much as I had.

Thanks to the archbishop's call for parishioners to take in or employ Irish orphans, Michael and some of the older boys had had little trouble finding employment — Michael with a carter. He said he wanted to earn his keep and put money aside for when Da got back on his feet. "It's a shame you cannot do the same, Johanna," he said.

"What about Uncle Liam?" I asked.

Michael managed to post a letter, but still has heard nothing and says that he does not expect word for some time, as this is a large country and the distances are great.

The man on the wagon called for Michael, and Michael said he must go. But he told me he would come again as often as he could and that if he found Da, he would get word to me. I hated to see him leave after so short a visit, but there was nothing to be done about it.

When I finished with the wash, I went and asked

Sister Marie-France about employment. She said that some of the older boys were finding positions as apprentices and some girls were being put into service. She offered to advertise for a position for me if that was what I wanted. I said I would be grateful.

### *July 14, 1847*

I slipped away again for an hour after I saw Sister Marie-France leave the house. We were supposed to be at contemplation, but I could not stop thinking of Da, and it is easy enough to steal away without notice. I was on my way to the sheds farthest from the road, which I had not yet been inside, when someone darted out and collided with me, sending me flying backward. At the same time, the boy — for it turned out that it was a boy not much older than I — dropped the bundle he was carrying. As I scrambled to my feet, the bundle, which was an old blanket, spilled out ragged clothing, a few bits of ancient cookware, a Bible, a purse . . . An odd collection of items, I thought. He jumped to his feet and began to cram everything back into the blanket. It was only when I saw him pick up a second Bible that it occurred to me what he was up to.

"You're a *thief,*" I said, scarcely believing the words even as I spoke them. "You're stealing from the sick."

He shoved everything into the blanket, grabbed up all four ends, and ran.

It took me longer than I would like to admit to come to my senses and to shout after him, "Thief! Thief!" But by then he had disappeared around a corner. I looked around for someone who might help, but there was no one. I went in search of someone in authority. When I finally found a harried-looking man and explained what had happened, he sighed loudly and declared that things would surely be different when the new sheds at Windmill Point were ready. And that was that.

I did not find Da or anyone who knew him.

### July 15, 1847

Grandda's words have been in my head all afternoon and evening. "Be careful what you wish for." To think I ever believed those words to be nonsense.

I slipped away to the sheds again, feeling emboldened by my success the past two times. Almost as soon as I arrived, I saw the thief who had knocked me down yesterday. He was skulking about outside one of the sheds, his eyes darting this way and that as he no doubt searched for what he could steal. I had to bite my tongue to keep from shouting. Instead, I bowed my head and made my way toward him, taking great care to circle around behind him so that he would not see me coming. I was very nearly upon him when he bent down and lifted what appeared to be a bundle of rags. Nestled in it were a beautifully carved brush and a comb of bone. He slipped both inside his shirt and straightened. That is when I grabbed his arm.

He spun around, his eyes wide at being caught. But when he saw it was me he laughed and twisted loose of my grasp as easily as you please. As he did, a small metal disc fell to the ground at his feet. I looked down at it. My head was spinning as I bent slowly to pick it up. It was then that he chose to run.

I caught the bit of metal in my hand and ran after him, determined not to let him slip away again. Someone let out a shout behind me, but I did not even turn to see who it was. I was too determined to catch the little thief.

He disappeared around a corner. By the time I reached it, he was a small thing at the end of the street and about to vanish again. Still I ran. At each turn I spotted him, only to have him disappear from sight. But I did not give up. I ran until I thought I would run the feet right off my ankles, and as I am taller than he and my legs are longer, I finally caught hold of him once more and this time I held tighter.

I held the bit of metal up to his face and, though I gasped for breath, demanded to know where he had got it.

"Found it," he muttered — and those two words shocked me more than I can say. 'Twas bad enough he was a thief, but he was also Irish!

"You should be ashamed of yourself," I told him. "Thieving from your own people."

"I only take from those who have no more use for earthly things," he said defiantly.

I was about to deliver him a lecture that would have made Ma proud when the meaning of his words struck me like a slap. I held up the small circle of metal dented on one side, the figure on it rubbed almost away, and demanded again to know where he had got it.

"From the same place as I get everything," he told me.

"And the man it belongs to?"

"*Belonged* to," he said.

How those two little words stabbed like daggers into my heart. I asked him to describe the owner, but he could not. So I was the one who did the describing, and the description I gave him was of my da. But still he could not say whether I was on the mark or not. I remembered the first poor soul I had seen and how I could not tell at first if it was man or woman.

"Was he wearing this around his neck on a bit of leather tied in four different places?" I asked, for that was how Da always wore his St. Joseph medal, on a bit of ancient leather that he had not been able to replace and that had broken several times.

The boy nodded.

"And you're sure he was dead?" I asked.

"As cold as the grave," was his reply.

I almost collapsed then. It was Da's medal — no doubt of it. It was his St. Joseph, the patron saint of carpenters.

He was gone. Da was gone.

I left the boy with his booty and stumbled back to the house, trying hard not to weep the whole way. I let myself in without trying to hide that I had been gone. What did I care about breaking some silly rules? I had not been an orphan when I first set foot in this house, but I entered now as one. Ma was gone and now so was Da.

Sister Marie-France appeared i the door of her office. Her face was sharp as she ld me that I had been missed. I think she would have scolded me but for my bursting into tears. She listened to my tale and then had another sister take me to the kitchen to make sure that I ate. She said that she would say a prayer for my da.

## July 16, 1847

I waited all day for Michael to visit and at the same time dreaded having to tell him what I had discovered. He did not come. This is not the great adventure I had expected. I wish we were still back home or at least that we had found a place to stay in England. Da was a fine carpenter. We would have found a way, and we would still be together.

## July 17, 1847

No Michael again today. I dread telling him my news, but still I wish he would come. He is all I have left.

## July 18, 1847

I was on my way up the stairs after mass with some linens this morning when I heard shouting in the front hall. My heart raced at the sound of the voice. I rushed, linens and all, to find Connor all wide-eyed and wild-haired, shouting, if you please, at Sister Marie-France. He had come for Daniel and was in a great temper to find that he had been given away, as he put it, to a farm family.

Sister Marie-France remained calm, although the flash in her eyes told me her patience was tested. She assured Connor that his brother was being well looked after and said, if he wished it, that she would send a message to the family to let them know that he would like to visit. This sent Connor's temper flaring again, for he did not want to *visit*. He wanted his brother *back*. Sister Marie-France was at her gentle best, saying that she understood how he must feel, but that the family who had adopted him had taken him in good faith and now must be consulted. She got Connor to agree to return in a week's time for an answer.

When Connor turned to leave, his eyes lit upon

me and a whiteness came over him. I took it as anger that I had let him down and began to apologize at once. To my astonishment, he rushed to me, took both my hands in his and held them tightly.

"I heard you *died*," he said.

"Whoever told you that?" I asked.

"Michael."

I was sure he must be joking, and said I saw no humour in the jest. But he swore to me that he had seen Michael only yesterday and that he was greatly saddened because he had learned that both Da and I had died.

It seems that Michael had done the same as I. He had gone to the sheds to search for Da. Connor said that he found a man who kept records of the patients, and that it was from this man that he learned that Da and Johanna Leary had died of the fever. The Johanna Leary in the record book had been brought to the shed only two days before Michael's visit.

"Where is he now?" I asked. I had to let Michael know that I was alive.

But Connor did not know. He and Michael met often in the square not far away, and he said he would look for him there tomorrow. He promised to send Michael to me. When I asked if he had had word of Kerry, he grew so sad that I felt sure the little lad must have passed. But, if anything, the news was worse: Connor did not know if his brother had died on Grosse Isle or if he had survived. If he survived, Connor did not know what had become of him. He planned to go back to Grosse Isle once he had Daniel in hand and the money for travel. He surprised me with a kiss on the cheek before he left, and said he did not blame me for what had happened to Daniel.

After he had gone, I begged Sister Marie-France to let me search for Michael. But I did not know where to find him or the name of his employer. In the end I had to agree to let her look into the matter.

### July 19, 1847

What a long and horrible day it was, and what a fine and generous person Sister Marie-France is. She went this morning to speak to one of the brothers who helps the older boys until they find employment. She was gone for the better part of the day. I watched for her constantly and rushed to her when I saw her open the gate.

She was not smiling. Her first words to me were, "I am sorry, Johanna."

I drew in a deep breath to prepare myself for what was to come, for if she had good news for me she would not say she was sorry and she would not have looked so sad.

The brother knew only that Michael had left his employer on a moment's notice. Sister Marie-France had also visited the sheds and had discovered that there is a Joanna Leary lately listed among the dead. The spelling is a little different from my own name, but Michael likely took this as a mistake if indeed he saw it written out.

I begged Sister Marie-France for the employer's name and asked where I could find him. She gave me the information and directions besides, and I made my way to the address, which was located down in a dank alley near the water. Mr. Stuart McEwen was a gruff man who grumbled about Michael's leaving suddenly. He did not know what had made him go so quickly, only that he was on his way to the Gatineau Hills, near Bytown. I guessed at once where Michael had gone. He is off to find Uncle Liam, whom he now takes to be his only living relative.

### Later

I have been sitting by the window and weeping over these pages all night. I begged Sister Marie-France to let me go after Michael, but the journey is long and difficult for a boy, never mind for a girl travelling alone. Sister Marie-France said she would write to inform our uncle that Michael is on his way. I asked for pen and paper so that I might do it myself. This surprised her. I do not think that she believed I could write. She agreed and promised to have the letter sent when I had finished.

How I ache to see Michael. And how I wish this country was not so big.

### July 20, 1847

Sister Marie-France sent my letter today. Now I have to wait, and I am not good at that.

I wish Connor would return so that I would have someone I know to talk to.

### July 21, 1847

Sister Marie-France sent for me late today. She has found me a position. My employers are to be Mr. and Mrs. Johnson. He is a businessman. They have three children. Someone will come to collect me.

### July 24, 1847

A man came for me in a wagon and drove me through the bustling streets, and everywhere I heard a language I do not understand. There are many people here who speak French. The driver, Pierre, is French but speaks English very well. He says that Montreal is home to more than fifty thousand people.

The houses are all of stone and have very steep roofs. Pierre says this is because it snows a lot in winter and the steep roofs let the snow slide off. If the roofs were flat, the snow would get very deep and the roofs might collapse. I cannot imagine so much snow.

At last we came to a large, handsome house. Pierre drove to the back and pointed to the door where I should enter. It led down into a large white-washed kitchen. A woman, her sleeves pushed up and a cap upon her head, set aside her rolling pin and came around the table to look more closely at me. She is Mrs. Coteau, the Johnsons' cook.

I dared not move as she circled me, even when — I am sure of it — she sniffed me and, sounding a wee bit disappointed, pronounced me "clean enough for now, I suppose." She then shepherded me up another much narrower set of stairs and along a dark hall to a door. She knocked, and a voice called, "Enter." A woman sat writing at a desk — Mrs. Johnson. She did not look up until she had finished writing, had dusted the powder off her page, and closed her account book.

Ma always said that you can no more judge a person at first glance than you can a pudding before you taste it, for people are often not what they seem. But she would change her mind if she met Mrs. Johnson. She is a thin, stern-looking woman. She is well-dressed and has her hair pulled back and held in place with silver combs, and I am sure there are many who would call her elegant. But her eyes spoil the picture. They are small and sharp and searching.

Mrs. Johnson sat back in her chair to inspect me. She did not address me but spoke only to Mrs.

Coteau, directing that I be washed thoroughly, for she did not trust the sisters to have done the job properly. After that I was to be shown my duties. Mrs. Coteau was to inform her directly if I was found to be unsuitable in any way.

I scrubbed myself in the kitchen under the eyes of Mrs. Coteau, who told me that "Madame" believed very much in cleanliness. She said that much of my time would be spent in the kitchen, but that I would be expected to help with the general cleaning when needed. I am to sleep on a small cot in the kitchen and to be responsible for stirring up the fire and boiling the kettle first thing each morning.

After I was deemed clean, I was put to work scouring pots with sand and then rinsing and drying them thoroughly. From the matter caked inside them, I guessed that they had been left where they were for a day or two. I later learned that I was right. Mrs. Johnson turned the previous girl out only two days ago. Mrs. Coteau had managed by using every vessel in the kitchen, praying that a replacement would appear before she herself would have to scrub the pots. Before I could finish this first chore, I was set to work on the vegetables for dinner. After that there was more washing up to do as well as finishing the pots. I scrubbed until my arms ached, my hands were as wrinkled as a crone's, and my feet felt like two great rocks. But I could not rest even then, for the kitchen floor had to be scrubbed from one end to the other.

I have found the perfect hiding place for my book and my bit of pencil. I have tucked them between the rope and the blanket of my little bed.

### July 25, 1847

Mrs. Coteau says I have got off to a bad start because she had to shake me awake this morning. No matter what I did — washing, scrubbing pots, preparing vegetables — she grumbled at me. For my part, I cannot believe that one household can consume so much food! For dinner there was soup, meat, bread, vegetables, relishes, pickles and pudding — but no potatoes. Mrs. Coteau, the gardener and I ate when the Johnsons had finished.

### July 26, 1847

Today was baking day. Mrs. Coteau bustled about, taking the bread dough, which she had set to rise during the night, out to a small bread oven behind the house. I was left to polish the silver and clean the knives, while watching a pot on the fire. It was so hot that I felt faint once or twice.

I caught sight of Mr. William Johnson for the first time. He is a banker. He dresses elegantly and leaves the house early each morning to go to his office. Mrs. Coteau says that he is an important man and that his business interests keep him busy, so he is not home for every evening meal. He is quite handsome and, unlike his wife, he smiles easily. The children ran down the stairs to greet him. The littlest one, whose legs still wobble when he walks, is a boy named Matthew. Mrs. Johnson immediately clapped her hands to shoo them away, saying that their poor father was too tired for such childish chaos. But clearly Mr. Johnson did not agree. "Nonsense," he declared, gathering Matthew and Nellie, who is seven, into his arms and carrying them up the stairs, trailed by Peggy, the eldest. I heard them laughing long after they had reached the top, and a terrible pain stabbed my heart. How I miss my own da and how he used to laugh and tumble with Michael and me and sing to wee Patrick.

## *July 27, 1847*

Cleaning, cleaning, cleaning. The most difficult are the carpets. Mrs. Johnson employs another girl, Claire, who clearly believes herself above me in station. Together she and I moved all the furniture so that we could take the carpets up one by one. We rolled them and took them outside, where we hung them on a line. I was left to beat them as if they were the most wicked creatures on earth and it had fallen to me to punish them. In the end, it was I who felt punished. No matter how long I pounded at them, it was deemed insufficient to shake loose every speck of dirt. I kept at it until I feared my arms would drop off. After I had beaten them to Claire's satisfaction, we dragged them back inside and replaced the furniture we had moved. My arms were so sore that I dropped two pots, one of soup and the other of gravy, one right after the other. Mrs. Coteau was very cross with me.

### July 28, 1847

Nellie Johnson came and stood beside me this morning while I hung out the linens. She has a head full of golden curls and the little pink lips of a cherub. She clutched a doll under one arm and watched me, feet firmly planted, for a few minutes. "Is it true you believe in fairies?" she asked at last.

I did not know what to say, so I asked her where she had heard such a thing.

"From Peggy," she said, meaning her sister, who is eleven and is like her mother in every way. "She says all Irish believe in fairies."

"Do you not believe in them?" I asked.

She shook her head but, to my mind, seemed to have doubts on the matter.

"Some people say that fairies are fallen angels," I said. "Do you know about fallen angels?"

Again she shook her head. Well, she is only seven and a Protestant to boot. I asked her if she would like to hear a fairy story while I worked. She looked up at me through thick brown lashes and nodded solemnly.

I told her the story of Lusmore the humpback and how it came about that he encountered some fairies and won them over with his beautiful voice and respectful manner. The fairies rewarded him for his singing and his courtesy by removing the ugly hump from his back. Another humpback heard of Lusmore's luck and asked him his secret.

Nellie's eyes were wide when she asked if Lusmore had told him about the fairies.

"Indeed, he did," I answered, "for he was a good and generous man."

But the second humpback was not like Lusmore. He interrupted the fairies when they sang their fairy songs and he was disrespectful enough to demand that they remove his hump as they had removed Lusmore's. His rudeness was rewarded: Not only did the fairies refuse to remove his hump, but they added Lusmore's to his back as well and he went away worse off than when he arrived.

"And that is why when you see a fairy or even think that one is about, you must always be respectful," I told her. "For fairies can be kind to those who are kind, but will punish those who are disrespectful or cruel."

She stared up at me for a very long time and then asked, "Are there fairies here?"

I told her I did not know, and that was the truth of it. She must have worried that there were fairies about for she thanked me sweetly for the story — *three times*!

### *July 30, 1847*

There are so many things to be cleaned in this house. There are dishes and pots and pans. There are cups and measures and spoons and beaters. There is cutlery. There are cloths and aprons and towels. There are tables and floors. There is the kitchen, the hall, porch, the stoop, the stairs. There are carpets. And all must be scrubbed or swept or polished until they sparkle.

While I was in the scullery with the pots, I heard Peggy outside, telling Mrs. Coteau about a new dress Mrs. Johnson was having made that she said was the latest fashion in London and that was to be trimmed with lace and beadwork. I thought how sad it was that my ma, who was much prettier and much sweeter than Mrs. Johnson, never had so fine a dress. Then Peggy told Mrs. Coteau something she had heard her mother read to her father from the newspaper. It was about how immigrants — the *Irish* immigrants — at the fever sheds were selling the bread and oatmeal they were given and were using the coppers they got in exchange to buy liquor!

She finished by saying that her mother says that

this proves they brought their misery on themselves. I do not believe a word of what she says. I cannot. I cannot believe that any of the people who were on our ship would do such a thing — nor any other immigrant either. The newspaper sounds as if it is written by an Englishman!

## *July 31, 1847*

Late this afternoon, while I was washing and scraping vegetables at the kitchen door, Peggy Johnson appeared, unnoticed by me until she demanded that I tell her a fairy story. She so startled me that I dropped the potato I was peeling and splashed water on the hem of her frock. She is tall for her age and ungainly, and has her mother's manner, for she regarded me with annoyance and said that I was clumsy. I think she will grow up with superior airs just like her mother. Her commanding tone is more than I can bear in someone who is two whole years younger than I am. I think that is why I chose to tell her the story of the Beautiful Maiden and her Three Aunts.

The mother of the beautiful maiden wanted so much for her daughter to marry the prince that she lied and told the king that her daughter could spin, weave and sew better than any maiden in the kingdom. The king promised that if the beautiful maiden spun a mound of flax into thread, made fabric from it and from that fashioned a shirt, the prince would marry her.

"I know this story," Peggy declared. "An old woman will do it for her and then the maiden must either guess the old woman's name or surrender her first-born child."

So smug did she sound that I was pleased indeed to tell her that she was wrong. I continued with the story, and she listened raptly despite herself as I described one old woman who appeared to spin the flax into thread, a second who made cloth of it, and a third who made a shirt of the cloth. All each asked in return was to be invited to the wedding when the maiden married the prince.

"But she did not invite them," Peggy declared triumphantly. "And they punished her."

"She did invite them," I said, pleased yet again to correct her. "And when the prince learned that the first one had such large and ugly feet because she spun so much, and the second was so fat because she sat so long at the loom weaving the thread into fabric, and the third had an ugly and bloodied nose from being stuck so often with a needle while she tried to thread it, he vowed that his bride would never have to spin or weave or sew."

Peggy stared at me for a moment. "I see," she said, still in her haughty tone. "So the lesson in the story is that if you lie about what you can do, you will be rewarded. I am not surprised." Then she added, "Mother says that Irish are lazy."

I was stung, but determined not to show it. Instead, I told her that I had heard the story from a woman who told it to her own daughter. That woman gave her daughter the following lesson: Unless you are beautiful like the maiden and have three fairy aunts, you cannot hope to be saved from hard work and how it wears on the body.

Anger flashed in Peggy's eyes. She opened her mouth to speak, but then plainly thought better of it, for she turned and flounced away.

After the evening meal, while I was elbow deep in soapy water, Mrs. Coteau told me that Mrs. Johnson wished to speak with me. I dried my hands and opened the kitchen door, and was surprised to find Mrs. Johnson standing right there in the hall.

"I will thank you to keep your heathen fairy stories to yourself," she said. "We do not abide such nonsense here. If I ever hear that you again speak to my Peggy as you did today, you will be dismissed immediately."

I was so stunned that I did not know what to say. Now I wish that I had found my tongue and told her exactly what I thought of her Peggy. But I did not. And perhaps it is as well, for if I am left alone in this world — as I fear now that I am in my little bed — I will have to depend on a good reference to find new employment.

## August 1, 1847

The Irish seem to be the talk of Montreal, and few have anything good to say. Just today I was in the scullery, dreaming of the delicious cakes and cream that Mrs. Coteau had made for company and wondering if any of them would return to the kitchen, even half-eaten, so that I might try one, when I heard voices. The kitchen windows, small and set high in the foundation wall, were all open so that we might have some air.

The voice was a man's, and I would not have paid attention had he not mentioned "the Irish." It was pitiable, he said, how they were heard to be starving in ditches. Then Mrs. Johnson spoke to declare that the Irish are lazy, adding that she had read in the newspaper an account of their sloth. She said that Irish children play in dung heaps and that the Irish are to be seen everywhere in the country with barely the clothes to cover their modesty, when moderate labour would easily procure them what they need. She called us "a nation of beggars and improvident creatures."

The gentleman protested that the potato crop had been ruined for two years in a row and that people were starving not out of laziness but from lack of food.

"They are lazy, ignorant creatures," Mrs. Johnson replied, adding that she spoke from first-hand knowledge. It took a moment before I realized that she was speaking of me. She called me "an ignorant thing who had never seen a cookstove before I charitably took her in and whose eyes grow as large as dinner plates at the merest mention of food."

She thought me ignorant? Poor perhaps. But never ignorant. Not I. I can read and write and do sums, thanks to Grandda, who was a schoolteacher in England before he came to Ireland and married Ma's ma, and thanks to Ma, who was not ignorant either. She loved her few books almost above all else. As for my da, how can you call someone ignorant when he is one of the finest carpenters in the county. Mrs. Johnson is the ignorant one for believing such lies!

It was then that I heard the gentlemen mention the fever sheds. "They are overflowing," he said. "The wretched souls who survived the ocean voyage are now dying in droves." To which Mrs. Johnson replied, "Their landlords should be ashamed of themselves for shovelling their problem onto our shores to be cared for by our charity."

I knew for myself that the sheds were filled with many decent people who had never needed any charity until they were forced to watch their loved ones die of hunger.

I despise Mrs. Johnson.

## August 2, 1847

More cleaning. Mrs. Coteau set me to work emptying shelves of pots and pans, scrubbing each shelf, washing, drying and polishing each pot and pan, and putting everything back exactly as it was. Mrs. Coteau especially emphasized that last instruction. She says she does not like to waste her precious time searching for items that have been misplaced. But there are so many things in this kitchen — a hundredfold and more than were ever in our own home. I was terrified that I would make a mistake and so, as I emptied each shelf, I stacked its contents exactly as they had been in their normal resting places and ordered them so that the items in the top shelf were stacked at the head of the table, those in the middle shelves were stacked in the middle, and so on. It was an admirable plan, for when Mrs. Coteau examined my work at the end of the day, she did not scold me. She only harrumphed and directed me to a new task.

## August 3, 1847

As soon as the breakfast pans were scrubbed I was set to work with Mrs. Coteau making sandwiches and slicing cakes. At the last minute I was called upstairs to assist Claire, who had been scolded for being overly slow in tidying the parlour and the front hall. Mrs. Johnson was to receive callers today. Everything had to be in perfect order.

Claire then put on her cleanest uniform and prepared to answer the door. I was sent to put out plates of buttered bread, cake and a large bowl of trifle that Mrs. Coteau had made and that smelled so delicious that my mouth fairly watered. I also brought up the first pot of tea and the first pitcher of lemonade so that Mrs. Johnson could offer her guests refreshments.

The house was fairly abuzz all afternoon with ladies coming and going. I was dispatched up and down the stairs to take up fresh cups, saucers, plates and spoons and to return back down the stairs with dirty ones, which Mrs. Coteau had me stack neatly on the sideboard. She would not let me begin to wash such fine china while she was too busy to supervise me.

It was only after the evening meal, which Mr. Johnson took but Mrs. Johnson did not, that Mrs. Coteau told me to fill some bowls with warm water and set them on the big table in the kitchen. She sat in her rocking chair mending tea towels while she watched me wash one cup at a time, and then the same with the saucers and small plates. I dried each one carefully, with much urging to be careful with each piece. Mrs. Coteau herself set them on their shelves.

## August 5, 1847

I am ashamed and glad both at the same time. I am not ashamed at being sent away, for I know I did nothing wrong. But I detest Mrs. Johnson and, as I left, wished her an eternity in the bad place, and for this I am ashamed. Da always said that there is enough wickedness in the world and, for this reason, we should leave evil thoughts to the evil and keep ourselves on the side of the angels.

Yesterday, after the fire was properly banked and Mrs. Coteau well tucked in her small room behind the kitchen, I hunted in my usual hiding place for my little book. *It wasn't there!* I looked again, thinking I must have misplaced it. It was not to be found.

I did not sleep even a wink last night. Thoughts of my little book filled my head. This morning when I took Mrs. Coteau her tea, my third chore of the day after stoking the fire in the stove and boiling the kettle, I asked if she had seen anything of mine lying about.

She gave me an odd look. "Anything of yours?" she said. "You had nothing when you came here but the clothes on your back, and those only out of charity." She told me to get to my chores. I thought about my book all day and wondered what had become of it.

After dinner when Mr. Johnson had gone to meet business acquaintances, Mrs. Coteau sent me to see Mrs. Johnson.

The door to the library was closed. I knocked and Mrs. Johnson bade me enter. Her face was as stern as Mrs. Coteau's had been when she sent me. She was holding a book that I recognized all too well.

"Explain this to me," she said, her teeth gritted as if to bite back her fury.

I could do nothing but stare at my book. What was she doing with it? How had she happened on it? I had left it in its usual place — between the blanket and the ropes of my cot. Mrs. Coteau had said that Mrs. Johnson never entered the kitchen. Yet somehow my book had ended up in her possession.

"You came here filthy, penniless, diseased, and yet I took you in," Mrs. Johnson said. "And this is how you repay me! How dare you write these things about me! How dare you presume to judge me!"

My mouth gaped. Not only had she taken my book, she had *read* it. She had read my personal thoughts!

Then she dismissed me. "You are to leave my house this instant," she said. "You are ungrateful and ignorant." She opened my book, grasping one half in each hand, and made ready to tear it in half. I didn't think about what I was doing. I lunged forward and wrenched it from her. She looked at me in astonishment. Her face turned scarlet and she slapped me on my face.

I didn't think. I couldn't think. I was too angry. She had wronged me. I raised my hand and slapped her back.

The room was silent. Mrs. Johnson stared at me, her eyes black with fury. A red welt the size of my hand appeared on her cheek.

"I could have you arrested," she screamed. "Leave my presence. Leave at once."

My legs shook as I left the library clutching my precious book. I went straight to the kitchen and stood there for a moment. I removed the apron I was wearing, folded it, and calmly set it on my cot. Mrs. Coteau watched me. She did not say a word. Taking only my book, I left.

I could not decide what to do. I had no friend in the city save Connor, and I did not know where to find him. I had no choice. I made my way back to the nuns, who took me in without a word. I am so grateful to them.

### *August 7, 1847*

Sister Marie-France sent for me at mid-morning. Her face was stern when she told me that Mrs. Johnson had paid a visit for the express purpose of lodging a complaint against me. She said that my actions displayed lack of gratitude and, worse, lack of humility. A person in my station could not afford to act as I had. Moreover, I did harm to other girls who had lost their parents and who relied on the charity of the sisters and the goodness of women like Mrs. Johnson who were willing to take into their homes girls who had none save the sisters to vouch for their character.

"What do you think would happen to other girls if ladies like Mrs. Johnson believed that they would all behave as you did?" she asked.

I had not thought of that. I know that a girl alone in the world, as I am, needs respectable employment, which they will never obtain if they have a reputation for making trouble or for bad character. I apologized for the trouble I had caused and said that I hoped I had caused no ill reflection on the sisters or their charges. Sister Marie-France bade me go to confession at the next opportunity and, in the meantime, to fetch a scrub brush and bucket and make the hall floor gleam.

When I turned to leave, she asked if it was true that I wrote every day in a small book. I felt my face burn, but I could not lie to her. When I said yes, she looked at me for a moment and said I would be better off using my book for reflecting on my own life rather than noting down gossip about ladies like Mrs. Johnson.

Hanging my head, I turned to leave. Sister Marie-France called me back. Her voice was gentler now, and she told me she had something else to tell me.

She had just this day received a letter that concerned me.

I whirled around, my heart soaring. It must be from Michael — or from Uncle Liam — for who else could it be?

Sister Marie-France's sad and sombre eyes dashed my hope to smithereens. The letter was from the postmaster in Bytown, near where my uncle lived. Uncle Liam has moved! He sold his land in the Gatineau Hills only a month ago and moved to where the land is even better. The postmaster knows the general area where Uncle Liam has gone and has written to another postmaster to find out for sure where he is. He will send word to Sister Marie-France as soon as he hears anything. He also says that Uncle Liam wrote to his brother in Ireland last autumn and feared the worst when he received no reply.

I reeled to hear this news. Why did Da not get this letter? Has Uncle Liam given up on us? Is that why he moved? And does he now, like Michael, believe me dead? And what of Michael? Will he be able to find Uncle Liam? What if he cannot? What will become of him?

But Sister Marie-France has already thought of that. She sent word to the postmaster to be on the lookout for Michael and to tell him that his sister is alive and in Montreal. She says that she will write to Uncle Liam to tell him where I am as soon as she hears from the postmaster in Bytown. She is so kind that I hugged her. Then, embarrassed, I pulled away from her. But she only smiled and said that she understood, for she had seven brothers of her own and were she in my place, she would worry too.

I thought to ask about Connor as well. Sister Marie-France had received word from the couple who adopted Daniel — they said they would be pleased to have a visit from Connor.

### August 8, 1847

I passed the evening with two other girls who were put out to service but had been sent back by their mistresses. Eileen, who is thirteen, was sent back because she kept breaking things, for which she was beaten. Mary Catherine, fifteen, was sent back when she fell ill. She is a thin little thing, all eyes and bones, and easily looks younger than her true age. She is better now that she is back with the sisters, but not strong enough to work yet. She has been told some charitable family will take her in but wishes to stay with the sisters. She says she wants to take her orders.

It was so nice to have someone to talk to for a change. That is one good thing about this house. But no one stays for long. You get to know a girl one day, and the next she is off to a new home or a new position. There is no chance of becoming dear and close friends who know each other like sisters, the way Anna and I did.

I wonder if Anna has made new friends. I wonder if she has forgotten me.

### August 9, 1847

Today would have been Patrick's first birthday. Ma would have fussed over him. Da would have danced him around the room. Da danced on everyone's birthday. I smiled as I pictured them and then — I could not help myself — I cried.

I asked permission to go to the nearby square where Connor had said that he and Michael used to meet. I thought I might find Connor or someone who knew him. Sister Marie-France let me go for a brief time after I helped with the laundry, but I might as well have stayed back. Half the people I approached had no English, and the other half knew nothing. I started to cry again, right there in the square.

How I wish that Ma and Da and Michael and Patrick and I were all together. How I wish we were back home, well-fed and happy, among our friends. How I wish things had never changed. Change brings nothing but heartbreak and sorrow.

### August 10, 1847

New children arrive almost daily and are in need of good food and clean clothes, so there is always much to do. I spent the day ironing and thinking about what Sister Marie-France had said. From now on, I will take her advice and try to use my book for reflection. My first reflection is this: I must pay far more attention to the task at hand when I am ironing, for heated irons are dangerous things. It is easy to burn a hand or the side of an arm out of carelessness when picking up a heated iron. It is easier still to drop a heated iron onto the ground, where it could fall upon (or, in my case, narrowly miss) the foot of some good sister who is going about her business. Also, it is astonishingly easy to let a hot iron linger a little too long upon an article of clothing or a crisp white sheet when the ironer (me) gets caught up in relating a story to another girl, and thus to leave a scald mark or even to burn the article right the way through. The sister in charge of the laundry said that we all learn best from our mistakes, but I can tell she does not relish having to report the loss of an otherwise perfectly good piece of linen.

Also, I am sure I do not know how the sisters bear the heat of the fire, the irons and the oppressive summer day in their woollen habits and wimples. God must truly love them.

### *August 11, 1847*

No news of Michael. I am beside myself with wanting to know.

Two of the sisters go each day to the fever sheds to care for the sick and the dying. I reflected a great deal on this and on what I saw when I went there looking for Da. I decided to ask Sister Marie-France if I might accompany them, even though she had turned down my request in the past. She wasted no time in saying no once more, but she was surprisingly gentle about it. She told me that many of those who are nursing the ill have sickened and died.

I reflected on that too and reminded her that I had not fallen ill on the ship or afterward, even when I visited the sheds against her wishes. I said that perhaps God had protected me because he meant for me to help the less fortunate of my countrymen. Then I told her what I had heard at the Johnsons and that Claire had heard Mr. Johnson say — that the newspaper reported every day the number who had died in the sheds.

"I want to help," I said.

She peered at me for a very long time and asked me if I understood the danger I might be in. I said I did. In the end, she said that I might go.

### August 12, 1847

Today I went to the emigrant sheds and worked side by side with the sisters. We did our best to give water and broth, when we had it, to the patients who are able to take them and, when we could, to move some of the worst-off patients onto clean bedding. But it was like trying to build a very long wall one small pebble at a time. I heard one gentleman tell another that there are more than fifteen hundred men, women and children in the sheds, and that some twenty or more die every day and must be disposed of. The same gentleman said that he will be glad when the new sheds are completed at Windmill Point and the sick are moved there, so that the plague which is carrying off so many of the city's "valuable citizens" may be checked and public confidence restored.

I did not understand what he meant by that, so I asked one of the sisters. She did not know either, but a doctor who overheard my question said that because of the sickness, business and travel about the city have suffered, and the city's merchants, save the coffin makers, are complaining that something must be done or the city will be ruined. The doctor spoke with a tone of disdain. He added that there are some people in the city who would like to ship all the Irish back to their landlords and would do it in a trice if there were a way that would not cost them anything.

### *August 13, 1847*

Da had always supposed that everything would be different across the ocean. But I am beginning to think that things are a misery for the least fortunate no matter where they may find themselves. Everywhere I go, I hear someone speak of the Irish as lazy and the makers of their own misfortune. But most who find themselves here are either ill or destitute through no fault of their own and have been reduced to beggary.

On my way to the sheds this morning, I saw a woman begging on the street corner. She told everyone who passed that she had two small children and that her husband and her third child had perished, one on the passage, the other in the sheds. A policeman came by, grabbed her by the arm and told her that begging was not tolerated on the streets and that if she was in need of something to eat, she should take herself to the sheds, where there was food to be had for the likes of her. She had no choice but to leave where she was, carrying one babe in her arms and tugging the other along behind her. I felt so sorry for her that I asked Sister if I could help her.

I picked up her little child and walked beside the woman, who was thin and haggard and looked as old as my ma, although she told me she was not yet twenty-four. She said that she did not know what was to become of her and her children. She had tried to find employment, but there was nothing save the prospect of going into service. She had considered that, even though it would mean giving up her children, but without any references and with no one to guarantee her as the sisters did me, she has had no luck. It does not help her case that she looks so ragged. I am sure many think she is diseased. I have heard that people are afraid to hire those from the ships for fear of contagion. At the same time, the city fathers worry that the many destitute will become a burden on the public purse. It seems an awful contradiction. People will not hire them even though they are in need of workers, and then they condemn the poor wretches for begging or for threatening to become a drain on the city's resources. It is as if people think the only way to solve the problem is to turn back time so that the Irish had not come in the first place. But that is not the way of the world.

I left the poor woman at the sheds, where she was told that there was no food to be had at the moment. The last I saw of her, she was sitting on the ground, both children gathered to her, her head bowed.

### August 14, 1847

I went to the sheds again. I make myself useful there, and it reminds me that there are many in this world who are worse off than I.

### August 16, 1847

Nothing much to write. I am so tired at the end of each day. Despite the sisters' best efforts, people continue to arrive ill and many die each day.

## August 19, 1847

When I am not at the sheds, I help the sisters with new young arrivals from the ships who either reach Montreal as orphans or whose parents are too ill to care for them. I help the little ones out of their rags and into a bath and fresh clothes. The older children seem glad to have someone from home to tell them about this new country. I also busy myself with laundry and scrubbing. In the evening, I help to settle the little ones. If they fuss, I tell them fairy stories in a whisper — the sisters do not approve of fairies — so that they will fall asleep. All the while I ache for news of Michael. I ache for my family — what little is left of it. I ache to be where I belong. And sometimes, late in the night, I awaken with an ache in my heart for Ma and Da.

## August 20, 1847

The new arrivals continue to be adopted by generous families. I see some of the men and women who come to take the youngest ones into their homes. Almost without exception, the women's hearts seem to soften as they bend down to look into blue eyes or brown eyes so close to the ground. Mother Superior insists that the babies be clean at all times so as to reassure those who are charitable enough to take them that they are not ill and carry no infection.

Older girls like me must earn their keep, of

course. It seems that we are regarded with more critical eyes and are quizzed as to what chores we did at home. I heard two women talking this morning as they waited to be admitted to the house. One said that Irish girls are little savages who are hopeless with housework and have to be watched every moment. "They are almost more trouble than they are worth," she said. And yet she had come to get a girl. The second declared that she would not take a girl unless she was satisfied that the girl would be of immediate assistance. "I have no time to teach an ignorant girl," she said.

### August 21, 1847

This morning I was sent to Sister Marie-France. My heart raced as I made my way to her door. Perhaps she had word about Michael. Or Uncle. My hand trembled as I rapped at her door. But when she called softly for me to enter and I let myself inside, my spirits sank, for she was not alone. There was a woman with her, a Mrs. Hall. She is English and, hearing of so many orphans advertised for service, had come to look for a girl. She has a gentle smile, clear blue eyes and a voice that sounds like a fine melody. She and her husband have been in the country only three years. They have two small children and need help about the house. She asked me about myself and my family, seemed pleased to learn that

I can both read and write, and, even though she is English, was sad to hear that all of my family save Michael perished with the fever. She seemed much nicer than the two women I overheard yesterday, and I was glad of the chance to earn my keep while I wait for word from Michael. At least, I was glad right up until she said that she would be leaving in four days' time to return to a place called Sherbrooke, which is several days' journey southeast of Montreal. When I heard that, all the gladness flew from my heart. If I leave Montreal, how will I ever find out about Michael and my uncle? That is why when Mrs. Hall asked me directly whether I would like to work for her, I hesitated.

Sister Marie-France quickly said that I was grateful for the offer and would be ready to do whatever was required. Mrs. Hall turned to me and asked if that was true.

I didn't know what to say.

Mrs. Hall said that if I did not want the position, I had only to say so. She said that she had a happy home but that she did not think it would stay happy if she employed someone who did not want to be there.

Sister Marie-France assured her that I had a good disposition and was a hard worker, but Mrs. Hall looked at me and waited for me to answer. I looked down at the floor and mumbled that I was happy to be offered a position.

There was a long silence. Finally Mrs. Hall said that she would return in two days and that if I was willing to go with her, the position was mine. If not, then she would interview another girl.

## August 22, 1847

I have thought of nothing but my uncertain future all last night and all of today. Tomorrow I have to give Mrs. Hall my answer. Sister Marie-France has said nothing, but I know she thinks I should take the position. But how can I? If I leave, how will Michael or my uncle find me? I do not know what to do.

## August 23, 1847

I made my decision last night. First thing this morning, I spoke to Sister Marie-France and asked her to write one more letter for me. Then, when Mrs. Hall returned and looked deep into my eyes and asked me if I was sure I wanted the position in her household, I said yes.

Mrs. Hall was not satisfied and asked Sister Marie-France if she might have a moment alone with me.

"Now then," she said when we were alone, "tell me what reservations you have."

I told her I had none.

"Two days ago when I made my offer, I was sure

you would refuse," she said. "Why have you now decided to accept?"

I felt I had no choice then but to explain why I had been torn between going with her and staying in Montreal. She listened to me without interruption. When I had finished, she said, "And now you are sure?"

I explained that Sister Marie-France had promised to write again to the postmaster in Bytown to tell him where I could be found. Mrs. Hall surprised me by suggesting I put a notice in the newspaper asking that anyone looking for me should inquire at the newspaper office, where Mrs. Hall would leave information about where I might be found. I said that this was a good idea but that I could not afford to pay for such a notice. Mrs. Hall said that she would pay and then deduct the amount from my wages.

She is so different from Mrs. Johnson that I can scarcely believe it. She knows nothing about me, but still she cares about my happiness and well-being. I mean to work hard for her and to be especially careful not to drop anything. I do not want her ever to be sorry for the effort she has made to help me.

### *August 25, 1847*

I went one last time to the fever sheds with the sisters. I put my arm around a girl no older than myself to help her drink some water. The straw upon which she lay was damp and putrid, but there was nothing to be done about that. Her gown, little more than a rag, was equally smelly, and she lay without so much as a piece of sheet to cover her.

"You are an angel," she managed to say after she had drunk her fill.

When I assured her that 'twas nothing but Christian charity, her eyes widened.

"You are Irish," she said.

I said that I was and that I had come to Canada for the same reason she had. She sank back against the filthy straw and said that she had imagined mountains of butter and rivers of milk. She had been told, as I had, that everyone in Canada eats meat every day and that honey flows in abundance. She asked if I had tasted these things.

I told her that I had had meat, milk and butter, but that I had not yet tasted the honey. She smiled and closed her eyes. I imagined that she was thinking of how sweet the butter would taste. A few moments passed, and the weight of her frail body grew heavy against my arm. I realized then that she had slipped away. I laid her down and went to tell one of the sisters, who sent me to put out fresh straw that had been delivered to the sheds that afternoon.

Along with some brothers, I began to remove some of the foul old stuff and replace it with the new. It was heavy work. I was pushing a cart laden with damp and heavy straw across the cobbles when I came to a jarring halt. One of the wheels had caught on a cobble that had worked its way up above the others. I pulled the cart back and tried to guide the wheel around, but succeeded only in coming up against another crooked stone.

"Let me do that," said a soft voice behind me. I stood back gratefully to let a lad guide the cart around the snag. Then, still holding the cart handles, he asked where I was taking the straw. When I told him, he pushed on. I trotted after him, grateful for the assistance. Only when I drew even with him did I see who he was.

"You're the *thief*," I said.

He did not seem in the least bothered by the accusation.

"I've a mind to call for a constable," I said.

He laughed and said that no constable would help me as he was doing, unless there was a profit to be made from foul and diseased straw, in which case, I would be relieved of both my load and my cart, and that would be the last I saw of either.

"So you justify your own thievery by accusing everyone of being a thief," I said.

"Not everyone," he answered. "Only those who deserve it." He grinned at me again, sassy lad. As we walked, he told me his own story. His name is Tommy Ryan.

After the potatoes had blackened, his da went

to work at road building in exchange for barely enough food for one person. He gave the food to his family, but it wasn't enough. Two little sisters died of hunger and fever. His da kept working until at last he, too, died from want of food. The landlord then drove the rest of the family from their home and put them on a leaky ship bound for Canada. Tommy's ma died of the fever on the ship, and he had made up his mind to rely only on himself when he finally landed, alone.

I felt sorry for him, for, like me, he had lost his family. "Still, it's no excuse to take what doesn't belong to you," I said.

"Like that medal?" he asked. "It was lying on the ground, I swear it. The man it belonged to had already passed."

Tears sprang to my eyes at the thought of my da lying in that terrible place.

Tommy touched my arm and asked if the man was a relation of mine. When I nodded, he said he was sorry and that if he had known that — and known me — he would not have taken it.

"So it's only *strange* countrymen that you steal from?" I asked.

He was silent, then after a moment he said that leaving home did not turn out to be the salvation his ma dreamed of. Nor his da.

That was true enough. He asked me if I was alone.

"I have a brother, but . . . " Tears stung my eyes. "He thinks I died in the fever sheds. I know he'd be looking for me if only he knew I still lived. And I have been trying to find out where he is. But I have found employment with a family near Sherbrooke. I'm leaving for there tomorrow."

We reached our destination at the water's edge. He lifted the handles of the cart and dumped the straw into the water below. Then he insisted on pushing the cart back for me. On the way he asked me to tell my story, and I did, from the time we set sail, to my time at Mrs. Johnson's, and my hope that Mrs. Hall would turn out to be a better employer.

"In my time here, I've met a lot of people from back home," he said. "What's your brother's name?"

When I told him, he said that if he ever saw Michael, he would tell him to look for me with the Hall family outside of Sherbrooke. He wished me luck and left.

### *August 26, 1847*

On my last morning in Montreal I packed my meagre belongings — my little book; a fresh stub of pencil that had been given to me by the sisters; an old apron and a worn coat, also gifts from the sisters — all caught up in a bundle and tied with strips of rag, and stood waiting at the gate early in the morning. I had said my goodbyes to those who mattered, not a soul among them kin to me.

A wagon came by after a while. In the front sat a man and a woman I did not recognize. Immediately behind was Mrs. Hall with two young girls. In the back was a third, older girl.

The man, the woman and the older girl were Mr. and Mrs. Fenton and their younger daughter Fanny, who is a year older than I. The two little ones were Mrs. Hall's children, Lucy, just five, and Catherine, not yet a year old and plumper than Patrick had ever been. Mrs. Hall smiled when she saw me. Mrs. Fenton sniffed the air when I was introduced, as if she expected to smell some unpleasant odour lingering on me. She told me that I might sit at the very back of the wagon. I climbed up and we were off.

We had not travelled far before Fanny crawled back to sit beside me. Almost instantly her mother called for her to come away. Fanny protested, but her mother's voice was sharp. Groaning, Fanny did as she was told. Mrs. Fenton did not lower her voice when she told Fanny that she should stay clear of me because I was one of "those Irish" who were spreading disease all over the city. Mrs. Hall protested and said that I was quite healthy, but Mrs. Fenton said that she was being foolish by taking someone like me into her home. My ears burned, but I kept my mouth shut and refused even to turn around and look at Mrs. Fenton. Instead, I pretended that I had not heard a word.

I watched the city fall away to pasture. It was late in the day when we crossed a bridge, and later still when the wagon turned off at the roadside, where we spent the night at what Mrs. Fenton called a most disagreeable inn. For myself, I found it not so bad. I helped Mrs. Hall with the little girls and slept on a clean straw mattress on the floor with a blanket to cover myself. We passed another long day on the wagon, and many times got off and walked where the road was bad or had been washed away. Fanny sometimes walked with me and Lucy. She chattered about her visit to Montreal and the pictures she had seen of the latest fashions in England, and did not seem to mind how quiet I was. I did not know what to say to her. In some places the road consisted of logs laid side by side, making it far too spine-jarring to ride. It is a wonder the wheels were not shaken off the wagon. At long last we found another inn, this one more to Mrs. Fenton's liking. She deemed it cleaner and the food more palatable. The next day Mr. Fenton left Mrs. Hall, the children and me at the Halls' house.

The house stands in the middle of a clearing. Mrs. Hall says that it took her husband and many men more than two years of chopping trees to make the clearing as large as it is. The house has two storeys, with stone around the bottom to as high as my waist and then clapboard the rest of the way up. The roof, like all roofs in this country, is very steep because of the snow. A veranda runs across the front of the house, and there is a kitchen garden at the rear where Mrs. Hall grows vegetables. She also gathers berries when they are in season and makes jam out of them. I have never tasted jam, but I did not tell her that.

The house is far from any town — it is a walk of several hours to get to Sherbrooke — or any neighbour other than the Fentons, but it is clean and bright and pretty. The walls in the drawing room are painted yellow and the window frames black. At the back of the house beside the drawing room is Mr. and Mrs. Hall's bedroom. Across from the drawing room is a dining room, and behind that another bedroom where Mrs. Hall's two little girls sleep. At the very back of the house is a kitchen that is as large as the one at Mrs. Johnson's house, but much sunnier, as it is not in the basement.

The second floor, which is smaller than the first, consists of three tidy little bedrooms, one of which is to be mine. It is scarcely as big as one of the cupboards in Mrs. Johnson's house, but it seems quite snug. And it is mine and mine alone! I can hardly believe it. The other two rooms are for the cook, Mrs. Lyons, and a man that Mr. Hall hopes to be able to hire for at least part of next year. In addition there are several storerooms where Mrs. Hall keeps trunks and boxes and Mr. Hall keeps scraps of wood, boxes of nails, and other carpentry supplies.

Mr. Hall came in before supper. He is a tall man, very handsome, with a trim moustache, soft brown eyes and an easy smile. He delights in his small daughters and Lucy clearly dotes on him. She laughs and giggles as soon as she sees him and runs to him, her chubby arms thrust up for him to catch her and hoist her above his head. He seems as eager as she is and happily obliges her.

### *August 31, 1847*

I have been so busy, there has been no time to write.

I slept three nights ago in my very own room for the first time ever with my very own bed and a mattress filled with straw. There is a big slit halfway down the mattress cover so that I can reach in and even out the straw when it gets lumpy. I also have linen and a blanket. When winter comes, Mrs. Hall says I am to have a quilt to keep me warm. She says it gets very cold in this part of the country and that it may come as a shock to me.

My head is stuffed with all the things I have learned. I have been left largely in the care of Mrs. Lyons these past days. She makes sure I pay sharp attention to everything she does and warned me that I must be prepared to work hard, for there are six men expected for the next several days to help Mr. Hall build a barn for his team of oxen, his four cows, his six sheep with lambs, and his pigs. At present they are occupying a small shed that he and Mrs. Hall lived in when they first arrived in this country. Mrs. Lyons says that these men will be very hungry and must be fed good wholesome food.

## *September 1, 1847*

Mrs. Lyons was right. The workmen are hungry, and they eat so much I can hardly believe it! They dined today on beef and pork with vegetables from Mrs. Hall's garden, a hearty pea soup, bread with butter, and tea with sugar. This will mean much cooking and baking, both on the cookstove and over the hearth. It is much harder work even than at Mrs. Johnson's, but Mrs. Lyons is much gentler than Mrs. Coteau, although she does seem particular about how she likes things done. She told me never to guess how a thing is done or where an item goes, but to ask instead. She says things will go much more smoothly if we pull in the same harness like a pair of well-trained workhorses.

In addition to the cooking, I have been helping with the little girls, especially Lucy, who is always eager to play chase-about. I am so grateful for my little room. I fall into my bed each night, so tired I cannot keep my eyes open.

## September 2, 1847

I am too weary to write.

## September 3, 1847

After the evening meal, Mrs. Hall asked me if I knew how to knit. I said yes, although I am not very good at it. I learned when I was small, but times got hard and we could not afford the wool. I am horribly out of practice.

Mrs. Hall gave me some yarn and some needles and asked me to show her some stitches, but I forgot how to cast on! My cheeks burned as I fumbled with the yarn. Finally Mrs. Hall said she would show me. She did not seem at all annoyed or angry. After that, I knitted a few inches. I was so nervous that my knitting got tighter and tighter, so that the square I was working on started to look like a triangle. Mrs. Hall laughed, but in a nice way, and said she used to have the same trouble whenever she worked with a new pair of knitting needles. She pulled out all the stitches and told me to start again. This time I cast on by myself and got it right.

## September 4, 1847

Mrs. Fenton and Fanny came to visit together with Fanny's elder sister Elizabeth, who married last year and is on her way to meet her husband in Montreal. While they sat and talked, I amused Lucy and Catherine. Mrs. Fenton criticized my work, saying I was allowing them to be too noisy. She spoke as if I were working for her instead of Mrs. Hall. I was glad to be sent to the kitchen to help Mrs. Lyons get tea ready.

Fanny appeared a moment later, and I braced myself for some new criticism. But instead she helped me with my work and asked me if it was true that I had come to Canada because of the famine in Ireland. When I said I had, she asked so many questions about my family and my life back home that it made me quite melancholy. I think she must have sensed that, for she changed her tack and said that she would take me walking one afternoon when Mrs. Hall could spare me, to acquaint me with the countryside. She seems nice and I enjoy her happy chatter. She reminds me a little of Anna, who was always full of talk, usually wishing for things she had heard about but never seen. (Most of all, Anna wished for a gown made out of golden thread.)

### September 6, 1847

I do not think that Mrs. Johnson would last even two days if she changed places with Mrs. Hall. Mrs. Johnson merely orders people about. Mrs. Hall supervises Mrs. Lyons and me, but she also works hard herself. This morning she sent me to the garden for vegetables. I took Lucy with me. She begged to help me, and I allowed her to do so even though I had to watch constantly that she did not trample any of the plants. When I returned to the house, Mrs. Hall and Mrs. Lyons had the bread in the bake oven, soup stock on the stove, and had started to prepare the meat for the workmen's dinner — and were keeping an eye on baby Catherine, who slept in a basket in the corner.

Mr. Hall works as hard as Mrs. Hall. For the past week he has been with the men raising the new barn. In the evenings — at least before the barn raising started — he works on some project or other. He is making a small chest of drawers, which Mrs. Hall says is to be for my use. I am knitting a simple shawl while Mrs. Hall cuts down an old coat for me. She says I will need both for the coming winter, and that the one the sisters gave me will not be warm enough. Mr. Hall also spares time for his daughters. When Lucy begs to be picked up or to ride him as if he were a pony, he obliges no matter how tired he is. He also picks up little Catherine and rocks her in his arms until she falls asleep. Mrs. Hall looks at him the way Ma used to look at Da before things got bad.

### September 10, 1847

The barn is finished and the workmen have gone. Mrs. Hall is greatly relieved. Not only was it unending work to keep them fed, but it was a great expense. Mrs. Hall calculates that they ate more than 150 pounds of beef in the ten days they were here and five loaves of bread every day in addition to buckets of soup and great quantities of butter and tea and sugar. Mr. Hall laughed softly as he often does and said that the new barn will pay them back a hundredfold.

I have started my very own quilt. Mrs. Hall has a great bag filled with scrap pieces of fabric. She collects them from the ends of clothes that she makes or remakes. On her last trip to Montreal, the one when she engaged me, she paid a visit to a woman who is known to her family in England. This woman gave Mrs. Hall a large sack of scrap fabric — torn and worn-out items of all kinds — in every colour you can imagine: red and blue and yellow and green, purple and pink. I am cutting out some pieces longer than they are wide and will stitch them in a pretty pattern.

### September 13, 1847

I don't know what has come over me. I have been melancholy since morning despite the brightness and business of the day. I have been thinking of Michael since morning and wondering what has become of him. I think also of Connor and wonder if he has seen Daniel or has discovered what became of Kerry. I wish Ma and Da were with me and that we had our own cosy house with a cow in the barn, and chickens, just like the Halls. Mrs. Hall says that with plenty of hard work, anyone can succeed in this country. No one is as hard a worker as my own dear da. He would have succeeded. I know it.

Today I helped with the laundry. Mrs. Hall used to have a woman come in to help her, but now she is teaching me. It is hard, hot work. Mrs. Hall says I must be careful not to waste any soap, for she had it made by a woman in the area. She supplied the candle stubs, grease from pot skimmings, and old bones. As payment, the woman kept part of the soap to sell.

Also, I have discovered the secret of maize. The Americans sent maize to Ireland for the starving, but it was so hard and difficult to digest that it made people ill. Now I know why. It was not properly prepared. First you have to boil the kernels. Then you have to drain them and dry them before the fire until the skin starts to split. Then you tie the maize in a bag and beat it with a stick — Mrs. Lyons showed me how — until the bran, which is the outside of the kernel, falls off. Finally you boil the maize until it is soft. The result is very pleasing, especially when it is served with hot milk.

### September 15, 1847

Fanny came today just to see me! Mrs. Hall said that she thought she could spare me for an hour, and we went walking in the woods together. Fanny started by showing me different trees and plants and telling me their names, but soon we started talking about other things. She is very curious about Ireland

and about what happened to my family. Before I knew it, I didn't feel shy anymore and was telling her everything — how first Patrick and then Ma had died, how Da had fallen ill on the way to Montreal, how I had learned of his passing, until finally all I had left was Michael. When she learned that Michael had left because he thought I was dead, she hugged me. And when, despite my best intentions, I cried for fear that I would never see him again, she hugged me even more tightly. She promised to come and visit again as soon as she could get away.

### September 18, 1847

I have started working on my quilt in my spare time. I can sew straight seams, as I often helped Ma remake clothes. But I have not done much fancy work and Ma usually showed me exactly what she wanted me to do. Also, the seams did not show, the way every single stitch on a quilt does. I find that my stitches are different sizes, which does not look nice. Mrs. Hall showed me how to keep them neat and small. It looks easy when she does it, but I have to concentrate very hard to make mine look as perfect as hers. Still, I know I am improving because at first Mrs. Hall tore out most of my stitches and said it would be better to start again. Now she makes little comments and corrections. I haven't had to tear out any stitches for days.

## September 21, 1847

A friend of Mr. Hall's sent over two bushels of apples. Some will be kept in a barrel in the root cellar. The rest had to be dried. Mrs. Fenton and Fanny came over to help core, peel and slice the apples and then hang the pieces on strings to dry. Mrs. Lyons says that in some parts of the country, apple-peeling is an occasion for get-togethers and merriment. She says girls try to peel an apple in one long strip and then throw the peel over their shoulders. Whatever letter the peel makes when it strikes the ground is supposed to be the first letter of the name of the man they will eventually marry.

Fanny said we should try it. Her peel formed an *S* or an *N*, depending on how you looked at it. We shouted out every name we knew that began with those letters, but Fanny rejected any boy she knew with those names and wanted to try again. It took me forever to get a peel off in one strip. When I tossed it over my shoulder, it made the letter *C*, and I thought immediately of Connor. I had a picture of him and Daniel happily together and, although I know it is wrong, I was jealous. Where is Michael?

## September 23, 1847

Mrs. Hall was busy all day nursing Catherine, who is feverish and vomiting. I have been too busy helping her to write more than just this little bit.

## September 24, 1847

Catherine is a little better, but she does not want to play. She clings to Mrs. Hall.

## September 25, 1847

Catherine is feeling better. Mrs. Hall is much relieved. So am I, for seeing the wee thing so ill reminds me of Patrick, and that reminds me how much I miss Ma and Da and Michael. Mrs. Lyons told me that Mrs. Hall lost her last baby, a little boy, to fever.

## September 26, 1847

A man I do not know came by yesterday and gave Mrs. Hall some letters and parcels from the post office in Sherbrooke. Mrs. Hall was busy putting Catherine down for a nap, so she set them aside without even looking at them. I was beside myself waiting for her to return to the parlour and go through the letters in case there was something among them from Sister Marie-France or even from Michael. But when she finally came back out of the bedroom, Lucy claimed her attention, and the little bundle of mail stayed where she had left it on a bench near the front door. I kept eyeing it and wondering if I should ask her about it. Mr. Hall finally came in from pulling stumps, saw it and sorted through it, calling out to

Mrs. Hall who each letter and parcel was from. I held my breath to the very end, hoping and praying. But there was nothing for me. I hid my disappointment and cried when I was in bed.

## *September 27, 1847*

I know it is probably a sin to say so, but I do not like Mrs. Fenton one bit. She comes to visit at least once a week, sometimes more often, as the Fentons are the closest neighbours to the Halls. She came today and, as is usual, Fanny came with her. She sat down in the kitchen with me while I cleaned the silver. Fanny is fun to talk to. She likes to read, and has an aunt in Boston who is well married and has a fine library of books. She is always sending books to Fanny, and Fanny always tells me about the latest one she is reading. She likes poetry best and has learned many poems by heart. She recites them to me. She also reads novels and books about explorations to distant parts of the world. She is reading one now about a Scotsman named Mungo Park who visited the deepest parts of Africa. It is a thrilling story. Fanny says she knows that he survived his expedition, for how else could he have written about it, but that she holds her breath at every turn to see how he will get out of some fresh new disaster. She promises to lend me the book when she has finished reading it, although I think by then that I will already know the whole story!

Mrs. Fenton must have been listening to us at least part of the time. Maybe she was even spying on us, for as soon as she heard me address Fanny as just that — Fanny — she became furious. She demanded that I address her as Miss Fanny and said that it was presumptuous of me — those were her exact words — to speak to Fanny as if she were my equal. Mrs. Hall said very quietly that she considered me a part of her family. I could have wept with joy. But Mrs. Fenton remained unmoved.

"And does she call you mother?" she said, more sharply than I have ever heard her speak to Mrs. Hall. What a ridiculous question! Even Fanny said so, but her mother silenced her with a cutting look. What a nasty woman!

Mrs. Hall said later that Mrs. Fenton has some prejudice against the Irish. She said there are many people who are angry that so many Irish have come to Canada, and that so many of them are ill and unable to look after themselves. She hastened to add that she is not one of those people and that she does not blame the immigrants themselves for their plight.

"You must not take offence," she told me. "Mrs. Fenton has strong opinions, but she is a good woman. I am confident that she would change her opinion of you if she knew you as I do."

For myself, I do not share that confidence.

## October 2, 1847

I am stealing a few moments to write before sleep gets the better of me. I have been so busy. In addition to my regular chores, I have been helping to prepare for winter. A cow and two pigs were butchered, as was one of the oxen. The meat all had to be stored. Some of it is being smoked and some is being salted. Mrs. Hall and Mrs. Lyons are making sausage, which I will finally get to taste. I wonder if it will sizzle. Mrs. Hall says that we will use the tallow to make candles. The hides of the animals are to be sold.

## October 3, 1847

Fanny came today to give Catherine a wee cloth doll she had made. But she confided in me that her true purpose was to visit me. She says she is glad to have a friend near her own age close by. A friend — that is exactly what she said! She brought me the book about Mungo Park and said I might keep it as long as I like. I wish I had something to give her in return. When my knitting improves, I will make her some warm socks for winter.

When I asked if her mother will be angry that she slipped away, Fanny said that she was sure to be. But she says that although her mother is often angry, she is more often quite pleasant and that I must not mind her, as she is not as harsh as she seems. She says Mrs. Fenton adores the little Hall girls, especially since

Fanny had a brother and a sister who died before Fanny was born. The little boy was five and the little girl was three. Fanny says this is why her mother finds every excuse to visit the Halls.

This gave me a different picture of Mrs. Fenton. She has more in common with my own ma than I had imagined. But she is different, too, for Ma treated everyone with equal respect while Mrs. Fenton puts herself above some, such as me. I do not think that is right.

### October 7, 1847

Today I made 50 pounds of candles! Mrs. Hall declares them to be the finest candles she has ever had. While it is true that she had to show me what to do, she did not have to stand over me while I worked. Indeed, she could not, as she and Mrs. Lyons salted over 100 pounds of meat.

Mrs. Hall was anxious about her candles. She bought molds for them while she was in Montreal, which she says make the job much easier than having to dip each candle in the hot tallow, then cool it, then dip it again and again to get it to the right thickness. Apart from the heat of the tallow, candle-making is easy. First you thread the wick, which comes in a ball, through the mold and tie it at the bottom. Then you pour hot tallow into the mold and set it aside to cool. It is hard to imagine any simpler chore.

### October 9, 1847

Catherine is fevered again and unable to keep anything in her stomach. The poor little thing has been putting up such a fight. I would never say so to Mrs. Hall, but she seems to weaken with every bout of fever. Her face is as white as Mrs. Lyon's apron but for the two apple-red fever spots on her little cheeks. She shows no interest in the doll or the corn-husk horses Lucy and I made for her. Instead she lies on the sofa and either sleeps, or gazes at her mother with dull eyes. The doctor has come again and has again prescribed warm baths. Mrs. Lyons continues to make arrowroot gruel, which Mrs. Hall tries to feed her, usually without much success.

### October 10, 1847

Mrs. Hall was up the whole night with Catherine. I know because I woke up twice and each time I heard her directly below me, singing softly while the rocking chair creaked. When I went down in the morning to stir the fire, the kitchen was already snug and warm. Mrs. Hall was still rocking Catherine, who was asleep in her arms. The worry and the pallor on Mrs. Hall's face put me in mind of my own ma when wee Patrick fell ill aboard ship. I miss them both, especially Patrick's merry gurgles, which never failed to bring a smile to Ma's face.

Before the whole household was awake, Mrs. Hall

slipped Catherine into her bed. She called in on her between each chore all day long. By mid-afternoon her worry had so deepened that she sent Mr. Hall again for the doctor. But he came back alone, saying the doctor had been called away to an accident some 10 miles to the north. A man was trampled by a team of oxen.

### *October 11, 1847*

The very worst has happened. I woke just as dawn broke, to a moan that put me in mind of the stories of banshees that Da used to tell when he wanted to make the hair on our heads stand up as straight as soldiers. It was Mrs. Hall. I didn't know what the matter was or what to do. I slipped out of my bed, wrapped a blanket around myself, and tip-toed downstairs.

The fever has carried Catherine off, poor little thing. Mr. Hall is as grief stricken as Mrs. Hall. Neither of them noted my presence. Mrs. Lyons had already put the pot on to boil. She sent me quietly to get Lucy dressed and dispatched me to get Mrs. Fenton. I got lost! I felt such a panic as I stared at the trees around me — they all looked the same. But I made myself sit down for a moment and told myself that I had walked the same route with Fanny at least twice and that if I concentrated, I would find the path. My heart beat very fast and my mind thought terrible thoughts, but I did it — I found the path!

Mr. Fenton drove Mrs. Fenton, Fanny and me back in the wagon. He went to help Mr. Hall, who was behind the house planing boards to make them smooth for the baby's casket.

Mrs. Fenton disappeared into Mrs. Hall's room, while Fanny did her best to amuse Lucy. I heard Mrs. Hall crying. Mrs. Fenton declared her intention to stay for as long as she was needed. She sent Fanny home and took charge, ordering both me and Mrs. Lyons about.

She was much satisfied with Mrs. Lyons but not at all satisfied with me. Nothing I do is fast enough or thorough enough for her. I don't mind so much as I used to. While I was sweeping the whole house with my cedar broom, I came upon Mrs. Fenton in the parlour. She was looking out the window, and when she turned I saw her wipe away a tear. She barked at me to finish my sweeping, but I knew she was only trying to hide her own grief at little Catherine's passing.

### October 12, 1847

Neighbours came all day to pay their respects. Mrs. Lyons kept the kettle constantly on the boil to make tea. I sliced and buttered bread and cut up little pieces of cake, some of it that Mrs. Lyons had made but most of it brought by neighbours who came to comfort Mrs. Hall. Mr. Hall was silent the whole day. Little Catherine lies in a coffin, which is lined with her own quilt, covered all over with roses and lilacs. I wish Patrick could have been laid out as prettily.

### October 13, 1847

Catherine was buried today on a little hill under an oak tree behind the Halls' house. Mr. Hall told Mrs. Hall that its canopy will keep the gravesite cool in the summer. Mrs. Hall stood on the hill all day until Mr. Hall went to fetch her back to the house. He sat with her and fed her the way one might feed a child. He told her that she must be strong, if only for Lucy, who is as quiet as can be and as pale as her mother. I think perhaps her parents forget that she, too, has lost someone dear to her.

### October 15, 1847

It is so quiet in the house. Mrs. Hall, who used to hum and sing for the little girls while she worked, is silent save for issuing instructions, and that she rarely has to do, for Mrs. Lyons knows her job well, and my routine does not vary much. Mr. Hall is out of the house from dawn to dark. When he returns, he plays quietly and wistfully with Lucy and then tucks her into her bed, which is now moved into the Halls' bedroom.

Since her sister's passing, Lucy refuses to sleep in her own room. She is as quiet as a wee mouse inside the house and speaks only when she accompanies me outside to replenish the kindling, to gather cedar boughs for a new broom, or on some other small errand. Then she begs me to tell her stories, which I gladly do, for the silence of the house weighs heavily on me. I think it weighs on Lucy too. I think she is silent because her parents are silent, and that she demands to sleep in their room to watch over them. I know she misses her baby sister, but I think she is more worried about her parents who are here and are so sad, than she is about her sister, who she knows is an angel in heaven.

### October 17, 1847

I wish my quilt was finished, for a deep chill has settled on us all and I could use the extra cover at night. It will look so beautiful on my little bed. I wish Ma were here to see what I have done — she would be pleased. I am using the colours of the autumn leaves before they fell — flame red, rich gold and bright orange. It will keep me warm all winter and I will remember the woods at their prettiest. Now the trees are bare and their branches reach up like the scrawny fingers of beggars pleading for a mouthful to eat or a penny to buy food.

After I finish my quilt, I want to make a small rug

for the floor of my room. It will keep my feet from getting so cold when I climb out of bed in the morning, and will brighten my room. I will make it out of scraps, like my quilt. Mrs. Lyons showed me how it is done. You cut strips of fabric and then stitch the shorts ends together to make long, colourful snakes. Then you plait the strips into a loose rope, coil them into an oval and sew them together. Mrs. Lyons has some old flannel that she says I can cut and sew to one side for the backing. She says she will help me as soon as she has finished the one she is working on.

### October 19, 1847

Mr. Hall went into Sherbrooke yesterday to sell the hide from the ox he butchered a few weeks ago. When he returned late this afternoon, he had a letter for me! How my hand trembled when he presented it to me! It was from Sister Marie-France. I stared at my name on the face of it for the longest time, unsure whether or not I wanted to open it. What if she had written with bad news? What if she had learned that my uncle had died? Or that something terrible had befallen Michael? But what if it was good news? Perhaps Sister Marie-France's letter had finally reached Uncle Liam. Perhaps the priest in the town near Uncle's former residence had encountered Michael and told him of my whereabouts. Perhaps Michael had returned to Montreal and seen the notice that Mrs. Hall had put in the newspaper, or had spoken to Sister Marie-France. Perhaps he was on his way this very minute to find me.

Mr. Hall spoke at last in a gentle voice and asked me if I wanted him to read the letter to me.

I shook my head. Whatever the news, it would not change because I was afraid to read it. I opened the letter and began to read Sister Marie-France's elegant script. My heart sank. The news was not the worst — there was no news of death. But neither was it the best news. Indeed, it was no news at all. To my shame, I found myself fighting back tears.

"Johanna, is everything all right?" Mrs. Hall asked.

I told her what the letter said. The priest had had no sign of Michael. Neither the sister's letter nor mine had produced any reply, and the newspaper that had printed my notice had received no reply regarding me.

"You have a home here for as long as you care to stay," Mrs. Hall said. Mr. Hall nodded his agreement. "You have made yourself a member of our family. I know Lucy would be heartbroken if you were to leave us."

I thanked her for her kindness. It is nice to have a place in the world. But how I wished that the news had been different! How I wished that my true place was with my brother and my uncle — with blood family. I tucked the letter in the pocket of my dress and busied myself with my work. I pulled it out again later, when I was alone, and reread it. This time I could not hold back my tears. Michael had been gone for so long without a word of news. Had he fallen ill, as Da had? Had some other misfortune befallen him? And what of Uncle Liam? Was I doomed forever to be a kinless stranger in this country? I wept until I fell asleep.

### October 21, 1847

While he was in Sherbrooke, Mr. Hall accepted employment from a logging company. He left today with two neighbours, Mr. Nearing and Mr. Webley. Men are needed to build a road for what Mr. Hall calls the winter sleigh haul. They will be gone for a few weeks. After Christmas the logging company will take them on again to transport the logs over the road to the edge of a river. In spring, when the ice breaks up, the logs are floated to sawmills or to ports to be loaded onto ships. The company pays cash, which Mrs. Lyons says is scarce but is needed to buy certain items.

Mrs. Lyons has also left for a while. She has been called to her brother's house to attend the funeral of her nephew, who perished after being thrown from a horse.

### *October 23, 1847*

There are just three of us in the house — Mrs. Hall, Lucy and me. I am grateful that Mrs. Hall is slowly coming back to herself. She even smiles from time to time, but not with the same brightness as before. I think she is remembering small moments with Catherine. The other day I heard her singing softly. It was not one of the gay tunes she used to sing, swirling around the room with one or other of her girls in her arms, but was slow and sombre like a hymn.

Mrs. Hall goes often to visit Catherine under the oak tree and sometimes sits and stares out the window at the little hill and the small marker on it. At least she has that comfort. I have none when I think of my dear ma and wee Patrick, who found their rest in the deep, dark sea. Nor of my da, buried somewhere in Montreal without a marker on his grave. I think of Michael and wonder where he is. I think too of Uncle and wonder what has become of him. Does he know that I am alive?

The air turns cooler every day. When my chores are done for the day, I sit with Mrs. Hall and work on my quilt. I am making good progress. Mrs. Hall is making long sturdy socks that Mr. Hall will wear when he goes about his winter work, which she says will consist mainly of working for the logging company. She says there is little besides that and indoor work that can be done during the winter months in this country. Mrs. Hall is also knitting warm stockings, mittens and a muffler for Lucy.

### *October 26, 1847*

Our days pass in quiet industry. I rise to a room so cold that my breath hangs in a cloud above my head. I dress quickly and steal down to the kitchen to stir up the fire and put on the kettle. I help Mrs. Hall prepare the morning meal. I sweep and wash and scrub. I play with Lucy while her mother attends to her own affairs. I help Mrs. Hall prepare the afternoon meal. I clean again. I work on my quilt and I learn from Mrs. Hall. She always has some piece of work to hand, and she shows me what she is doing and how it is done. She says that once all preparations are made for winter, she will help me cut down an old dress of hers to remake into one for me. She will show me every step so that I will learn what she says is important for any woman to know.

### *October 28, 1847*

Fanny came over today to lighten the workload and brighten the mood of the house. Here is something I did not know about her. Not only does she love to sing, but she has a beautiful voice! She taught Lucy and me some songs with different parts, and when we sang them together, Fanny taking one part and Lucy and I the other, Mrs. Hall declared that we sounded like a choir of angels. She even joined in, taking a third part, when we sang the song again. It was the happiest day the house has seen in a long time.

### October 31, 1847

Hallow Eve. It makes me homesick to remember the bone fires that would burn at home. It makes me miss Grandda too. He loved to tell stories on Hallow Eve about the spirit world and the fires that warmed wandering souls. He never minded the priests when they scolded him for such talk.

### November 4, 1847

Mrs. Lyons has returned. Mrs. Hall was so glad to see her that she hugged her. So did Lucy. I would have hugged her as well, but I was too shy.

Her return will brighten the days. It has been so cold that the windows are frozen over and it is impossible to see through them. The water in the little jug in my room is frozen solid when I get out of bed in the morning and the edge of my blanket is covered in ice where my breath freezes on it. We are all wearing shawls and blankets over our clothes to keep warm. Mrs. Hall made a bed on the sofa for Lucy and she played quietly under her blankets all day.

Mr. Fenton, who dropped by yesterday, said that he doesn't remember such cold so early in the season. But he said it was not as bad as one year early in his marriage when he was in his workshop making chairs for the parlour. So frigid was it that a nail froze to his bare hand before he could hammer it into the piece of wood he was working on. He tore the skin getting it off, and Mrs. Fenton had to bandage it. Fanny says that ever after, her mother cautioned him to wear mittens while working with nails during winter.

## *November 6, 1847*

The sky was as grey as stone yesterday morning, but the air was not as cold as it has been. Mrs. Lyons said that this was because it was going to snow. Sure enough, by mid-morning the sky was thick with fluffy flakes. They wafted down slowly and landed as lightly as if they were feathers. I bundled Lucy up and we went for a walk around the yard.

By midday the snow was up to the middle of my calf and was falling more thickly than ever. It snowed all day. At night the wind came up and blew the snow everywhere. When I arose this morning and went down to the kitchen to stir up the fire, I could not see out the kitchen window. I confess that I panicked. I thought that so much snow had fallen that the house was buried and that we would never get out nor anybody get in. Then Mr. Fenton came through the front door. He had come to check that all was well in Mr. Hall's absence and laughed to see me so obviously relieved. He took me to the veranda to show me that the snow was so high only on the north side of the house where the kitchen is and on the north side of the barn. This is because the wind blew from the north and gusted the snow. Where it could not be blown, it piled up in high drifts. How quiet and mysterious a house seems when it is cocooned in the white stuff.

### *November 10, 1847*

Mr. Fenton and Fanny drove over in a cutter to take Mrs. Hall, Lucy and me for a ride. He bundled us all up under a great bearskin to keep us warm and we flew off across the snow. The horses' breath drifted back in clouds toward us. Fanny taught me a song about sleigh-riding that she says is quite popular. We saw tracks in the snow — Mr. Fenton says they are deer. And all the trees — those without leaves and those that are always green — were frosted with snow. Everything was so pretty. We came back with apples in our cheeks and all feeling merry, and Mrs. Lyons had hot tea and bread and butter for us all.

### *November 14, 1847*

Lucy was restless today, and no wonder. Mr. Hall is due back any day. Lucy runs to the door constantly to see if she can catch a glimpse of him. Mrs. Hall has been feeling poorly for the past two days, so when Mrs. Fenton came to visit yesterday, she decided to stay. This put Mrs. Lyons's nose out of joint. She muttered to herself for much of the morning. She thinks she is quite able to look after Mrs. Hall and feels that Mrs. Fenton does not trust her to do so.

Mrs. Fenton told us both that Mrs. Hall is in a nervous state. Because of this she has forbidden any noise. She will not let me take Lucy outside, saying I am needed to mind my chores. Poor Lucy chafes for something to do. So this afternoon when Mrs. Fenton and Mrs. Lyons were busy in the kitchen, I told Lucy some fairy stories. To give her greater pleasure, I acted out the parts. I was careful to be quiet, telling Lucy that it is the custom to tell these stories in a low voice so that the fairies would not overhear them and become angry. She fell easily into the small ruse.

I told her three stories, then said I must get back to work. Lucy begged me for another. Just one more, she said, and she would be satisfied. So I began a story about the leprechauns and their pots of gold. At that Lucy jumped up and ran to the little desk that Mrs. Hall uses to write letters to her family. She opened one of the drawers and brought back a gold chain with a small but solid-gold pendant at one end.

"It's from Papa's watch," she said. "Grandfather gave it to him, but he says it's too grand to wear. It can be the gold in the leprechaun's pot."

I did not think this was a good idea, for it was

clear the watch fob was of great value. I told her to put it back. Disappointed, she started back to the desk to do as she was told. But in her haste, she tripped and the chain and fob flew from her hand and landed under the sofa. When she went to fetch it, she couldn't seem to get it. "It's stuck," she said. She pulled harder and then let out a yowl. She had tugged too hard and the golden fob separated from the chain. She thrust them into my hands just as Mrs. Fenton appeared, drawn by Lucy's cry.

"What on earth is going on? Did I not tell you to be quiet?" she hissed.

I glanced at Lucy, who was staring wide-eyed at Mrs. Fenton's angry face.

Mrs. Fenton stared at the golden chain and fob in my hands and then at the open desk drawer. She snatched them from my hands and demanded to know what I was doing.

"We were playing — " I began.

"You were stealing, and don't deny it," Mrs. Fenton said. Her face was as black as the sky when a storm strikes.

I tried to explain, but she wouldn't even let me start.

"Just as I have always suspected," she said. "You people are no better than animals." She said that she had warned Mrs. Hall not to take on an Irish girl because the Irish are lazy beggars. She threatened to tell Mrs. Hall what I had done, and said that I would be dismissed.

I was so angry at the slanders that my voice trembled when I told her that I would never steal from the Halls and that we were merely playing.

She slapped me. Her open hand struck my cheek with a sound like the report of a gun. She told me to gather my things, for I was dismissed immediately. Lucy began to cry. I think she was afraid that Mrs. Fenton would strike her too. I touched the spot where Mrs. Fenton had struck me — it was on fire — and told Mrs. Fenton that it was not her place to dismiss me. Her face grew even darker. I was sure that when next she spoke, thunder would echo out of her mouth and lightning bolts would flash from her eyes.

Mrs. Hall appeared at that moment and asked what the matter was. Lucy ran to her, crying, and wrapped her arms around her mother's legs, sobbing that Papa would be angry when he saw his watch chain.

"Johanna took it and broke it," Mrs. Fenton said. She held it up so that Mrs. Hall could see it. Mrs. Hall asked me if this was true. I didn't want to lie to her, but neither did I want Lucy to take the blame for something that was an accident. So I told Mrs. Hall that no harm was meant.

Mrs. Hall frowned. She looked at her sobbing daughter. Finally she knelt down before the child and made Lucy look into her eyes and swear to tell the truth. Tears rolled down Lucy's cheeks as she spilled out the whole story. Mrs. Hall thanked her for telling the truth and said that she must not touch Papa's things again. Then she scooped Lucy into her arms and comforted her. She suggested we all have a cup of tea and sent Mrs. Lyons and me to the kitchen to prepare it. Not another word was said about Mrs. Fenton's accusations.

Later Mrs. Lyons told me that Mrs. Fenton was not a bad person, but that she is forgetful about her own past. When I asked what she meant, she told me that Mrs. Fenton's father had brought the family from New York to Upper Canada after the American War of Independence. He was given land and three years' supply of food by the Crown. After the three years, there was a terrible drought, and all the crops failed. Mrs. Lyons said that Mrs. Fenton's family and many others tried to sell parts of their land for a few barrels of flour, but found no buyers. Others ate dogs and grew fond of the taste.

"To hear Mrs. Fenton tell it, sheer grit and determination got them through that terrible year," Mrs. Lyons said. "A year which, she never omits to mention, was no fault of their own. So next time she lays into you, Johanna, think of her father gnawing the bone of some poor dog. 'Twill make her seem less daunting."

Today Mrs. Lyons became a dear friend.

### *November 16, 1847*

Mrs. Hall is at the window as often as Lucy. I think she is worried that Mr. Hall has not returned yet. The house is not the same without him. But she is feeling stronger and sits with us in the evening instead of retiring early. Sometimes we tell stories. Mrs. Lyons tells about the early days in this country. Her great-grandparents were French and settled in what was then New France. Her grandmother caused a scandal by wedding an Englishman and raising her children in the English language. Mrs. Lyons also has stories about the Cree, stories that came to her from her grandmother, who heard them from *her* father, who was a fur trader. Even Mrs. Hall joins in with stories of some of the English kings.

Last night while Mrs. Lyons was working on some clothes for the expected babe of a niece in Montreal and Mrs. Lyons and I were knitting socks — she for Mr. Hall and I finishing a pair for Fanny — Lucy asked me to tell a fairy story. I shook my head. While children enjoy my stories, grown-ups in this country do not seem to approve. But Mrs. Hall said that she would love to hear one, so I launched into the tale of the vain princess who refuses all suitors as not being grand enough or handsome enough for her. At last her impatient father marries her off to the ugliest and lowliest man in the kingdom. He takes her to his wee den of a home where she is hard put to keep it clean and tidy and must learn to cook his meals without burning them and darn his socks without pricking herself and bleeding on them. At first she is resentful at her fall from grace. She refuses to kiss her own wed husband but instead puts him off with her haughty ways. But time goes by and she learns that her husband is a good and patient man when she is a good and patient wife. She learns too that he is so wise that people from all around come to him with their problems and he solves them all in a fair way that pleases all parties. To her great surprise, she falls in love with him. And one night when he would kiss her, she lets him. Before her very eyes he is transformed into the most handsome gentleman she has ever seen. The very next day, she learns that he is no rude peasant but is the master of a vast domain and that all the people who came to him with their problems are his subjects, who adore him.

"But why didn't you tell me?" she asked him.

"Because I wanted you to love me for myself," he replied, "and not for what I possess or how I look."

Lucy was pleased to learn that the two lived happily ever after and had two lovely daughters and two brave sons. Even Mrs. Hall and Mrs. Lyons sighed contentedly at the ending.

## November 19, 1847

It is nearly one month since Mr. Hall went away to the logging camp. The sky was leaden all day, and there was something ominous in the air. Mrs. Lyons said it was a storm brewing, but when I went outside to get more wood for the fire, it was as still as if the air had been sucked out of all life in the area. I hastened back inside.

The evening was starless because of the clouds, and there was no moon to be seen. The dishes had been washed and cleared away and the floors swept. The house was silent. Lucy had been out of sorts all day, so Mrs. Hall put her down in her own bed. Mrs. Lyons and I expected her to come back, but she did not. At last Mrs. Lyons tiptoed to the threshold, and a smile appeared on her lips.

"They are asleep in each other's arms," she said. "I think maybe the new child will make things easier on her."

"New child?" It took me a minute to understand that a new babe was on its way. I had had no inkling. Mrs. Lyons smiled and nodded. I hoped it would bring a fresh smile to Mrs. Hall's face.

Mrs. Lyons asked me to tell her a story. I was well into one about a leprechaun when, of a sudden, the very blood in my veins turned to ice and I stopped the tale, for didn't I hear the wail of the banshee? Mrs. Lyons said I looked as if I'd seen a ghost. Just then something crashed to the floor. It was a small likeness of Mr. Hall's mother. I stifled a scream, for everyone knows that when a picture falls off the wall, it foretells a death. And with the wail of the banshee I had heard . . .

Someone was going to die. I knew it in my heart. But I did not say a word to Mrs. Lyons for I did not think she would believe me.

### *November 20, 1847*

I was right. Someone *had* died. And Mr. Hall has been very badly injured. Here is what happened.

This morning, shortly after I had stirred the fire, I heard a noise, a whinny. I was sure of it. And right enough, when I looked outside, I saw a man in a sleigh turning off the road in the distance and making toward the house. I ran to get Mrs. Hall and found her at the window in the front room. She had seen the sleigh as well. As first she looked merely puzzled, wondering no doubt about the identity of the visitor. But her look of expectation turned to a frown and I heard her say, "It's Frederick Nearing. But where is — " She stopped before she finished her question. I cannot be sure, but I think she spotted what I had seen — a large bundle in the sleigh. Without stopping to protect herself against the cold, she ran out into the yard. Mrs. Lyons grabbed a shawl — as did I — and ran after her.

Mr. Nearing pulled up the sleigh and gazed down at Mrs. Hall. He looked weary as he said, "There was an accident."

Mrs. Hall moaned and reached for the blanket-wrapped bundle, which, I now saw, was as big as a man. But Mr. Nearing grabbed her hand before she could lift the blanket.

"It's Duncan Webley under there," he said gently.

He and Mr. Hall had been in an accident at the logging camp. Mr. Webley is dead, and Mr. Nearing was on his way to tell Mrs. Webley. Mr. Hall is in Sherbrooke, alive but badly hurt. Mr. Nearing said he would call back for Mrs. Hall after he visited Mrs. Webley, and would take her to Sherbrooke.

I am ashamed to say that I was relieved that the death that had been foretold was not Mr. Hall's. Mrs. Hall hurried inside to prepare for her trip.

### November 21, 1847

Mrs. Hall has gone to Sherbrooke, leaving Lucy in the care of Mrs. Lyons and me. When Mr. Nearing came back to get her he told us more about what had happened. He said that the demand for timber is so great in Europe that the men were pressed to work well into the evenings, piling up logs by the light of fires. He also says that many of the men are new to timbering and that, because of this, there are many accidents.

Mr. Hall was returning to camp when he saw two other men — Mr. Webley was one of them — piling logs. Mr. Webley turned to greet him. He did not notice when one of the logs, then the rest, started to roll toward him. But Mr. Hall saw. He shouted to the two men. The first bolted out of the way, but Mr. Webley did not understand what the problem was. Mr. Hall raced forward to try to push him aside. He failed. The logs fell on top of Mr. Webley, killing him almost at once. Some fell on top of Mr. Hall too, pinning him to the ground and crushing the right side of his body. Mr. Nearing said that he was lucky to be alive, although he confided to Mrs. Lyons and me that his arm is very bad and that he might lose it. Mrs. Lyons wept when she heard this. She thinks the world of Mr. Hall.

### November 30, 1847

Mrs. Lyons and I have been carrying on these past few days, keeping the house clean and snug and amusing Lucy with games and songs. She asks constantly for her parents. She has never been separated from both of them at the same time. Indeed, I find it strange to be here without them.

### December 1, 1847

This morning we were all in the kitchen — Mrs. Lyons was making soup, and Lucy was helping me measure flour for some bread — when I heard a distant jingle. I looked up and saw that Mrs. Lyons had an ear cocked to the window. So did Lucy. We all three rushed to see who it was. Lucy was the most excited, as she was sure it must be her ma and da. But it was not. It was Mr. and Mrs. Fenton and Fanny. They were solemn-faced when they came into the house. Mrs. Lyons offered to make some tea, and Mrs. Fenton accepted, but Mr. Fenton said that he could not stay. He looked uncomfortably at Mrs. Fenton, who told Fanny to take Lucy into the kitchen to see if there was any cake. After they had gone, Mrs. Fenton told us the news.

They had received word from Mrs. Hall. Mr. Hall is very badly injured. His leg has been broken in many places, and his arm so badly crushed that it became infected and the doctor had had no choice but to amputate it. Mrs. Lyons gasped when she heard this, and I felt hot tears run down my cheeks. Mr. Hall was never idle. He always kept himself busy, working to improve his farm. In the evening he liked nothing better than to work on a new piece of furniture and decorate it with patterns he cut into the wood. How would he be able to do that with one arm? How would he manage all that had to be done about the place with one arm?

Mrs. Fenton said that the Halls are not going to return home immediately. They plan to stay in

Sherbrooke until Mr. Hall is strong and able to get around. They want us to take Lucy to Sherbrooke.

Mr. Fenton is to drive us there in two days' time. Mrs. Fenton and Fanny will come back to help me pack what is needed. Mrs. Hall sent a list. Mr. Fenton will keep an eye on the house and the farm until the Halls can return.

### December 2, 1847

Fanny and Mrs. Fenton returned today. Fanny made up a song about packing that she and Lucy and I sang while we packed Lucy's things. Fanny kept Lucy busy while I gathered my belongings. I have more than I had when I arrived only a few months ago. I have my quilt, which is nearly finished, and the scraps of fabric for my little rug, which I intend to work on in my spare time. I also have the coat Mrs. Hall cut down for me, and an old pair of her boots that she gave me. And I have my shawl. And, of course, my book, with almost all of its pages filled now with so many sad things and so many new things. I will have to think what to do once I have filled it up.

After packing, I took a last look at my room. I was sorry to leave my bed and my little chest of drawers. They are the first pieces of furniture I've ever had to myself. But they will be here for me when I return.

I have decided to give my shawl to Fanny. It is

warm, and all the rows are even. I wrapped it in a bit of cloth, tied it with a twine bow and set it on a chair at the ready.

Mr. Fenton came before dark to take Mrs. Fenton and Fanny home. He says he will come to get us first thing in the morning so that we can set out for Sherbrooke.

I felt tears gather in my eyes when he said it, and Fanny slipped an arm around my waist and said she would miss me. A few tears slipped down my cheek when I said I would miss her too. It was as hard to say goodbye to her as it was to Anna. Fanny is my first true friend in Canada.

I brought out my package and presented it to her. She unwrapped it eagerly and was not at all disappointed. She declared that it was the finest shawl she had ever seen and wrapped it around her shoulders. Even Mrs. Fenton said that it was well-made. Then Fanny reached into her pocket and brought out a little package for me. When I opened it I could hardly believe what I saw. It was a brand new little book filled with blank pages.

"Mrs. Hall said that you like to write things down," she said. I felt my cheeks burn. Sister Marie-France must have told Mrs. Hall about how and why Mrs. Johnson had dismissed me. Fanny hugged me again and said she hoped that I would write to her, and that she would write to me too and would count the days until I returned with the Halls.

Tears trickled down my cheeks as I watched her drive away with her parents. I waved until she was out of sight and called goodbye until my throat was sore.

### December 3, 1847

Mr. Fenton arrived bright and early as he had promised, and loaded Lucy, Mrs. Lyons and me into the sleigh with all our bundles. The day was cold but bright and the snow hard and crisp under the runners of the sleigh. Mr. Fenton seemed pleased with our progress. For my part, I was happy to reach Sherbrooke.

The Halls have rented some rooms in a house in town. Mrs. Hall greeted us at the door. She scooped Lucy into her arms and covered her with kisses. But in reply to Lucy's demands to see her father, Mrs. Hall said she must wait, for her father was sleeping.

Mr. Fenton did not stay, for he wanted to return home before dark. Before he drove away, I asked him to watch for any letter for me at the post office in Sherbrooke. He said that he would, and truly astonished me by grasping my hand and wishing me good luck and saying that he hoped I would be reunited with my brother. Fanny must have told him. It was the first time Mr. Fenton has said anything to me, for he is a quiet man.

## December 4, 1847

I have not seen Mr. Hall yet. Mrs. Hall says that he does not feel up to visitors, although Lucy was allowed to sit with him for a few minutes.

Mrs. Hall is pale and her face lined with worry. As soon as Lucy was in bed, Mrs. Hall asked to speak to me. Mrs. Lyons was with her. Her tone was sombre when she said it was clear that they could not soon return to Sherbrooke and farming and, for that reason, she had to let one of us go. I looked down at my feet and prepared myself for what was to come. But it is Mrs. Lyons who is to leave, not me.

"Oh no," I said. It wasn't right that Mrs. Lyons should go and I should stay. "Let it be me," I pleaded. "Mrs. Lyons has been with you longer than I have. And she can cook!"

Mrs. Lyons laid one hand on mine and smiled at me. She said that she had already spoken to Mrs. Hall. She had received word a month ago that a favourite niece in Montreal was expecting and would welcome her help with the new baby. She had been wishing she could go, but was reluctant to leave Mrs. Hall. But now that things had changed, she was free to be with her niece and to welcome the new babe. She said she knew I would be a great help to Mrs. Hall, for I had learned a lot. Besides, she added, I was alone in the world, and that wasn't right. Mrs. Hall not only needed me with her, but she also wanted me to stay, and Mrs. Lyons was glad for that.

Mrs. Hall agreed and said that she truly needed me. I was almost in tears, torn between the kindness they both showed to me and the loss of Mrs. Lyons, who has been such a good friend.

Mrs. Lyons will leave in a few days' time.

### December 6, 1847

Mrs. Lyons left today. She gave me a beautiful handkerchief that she had embroidered with autumn leaves, for she said she knew how I loved the colours. She said that she hoped to visit one day and to sample a meal that I had made. I hugged her, and she hugged me back. I will miss her.

### December 7, 1847

Mrs. Hall had to run some errands today and took Lucy with her. She said that Mr. Hall was asleep, so there was nothing for me to worry about. I was sitting on a sofa knitting when I heard a terrible crash. It had come from the sick room. I rushed in and saw water all over the floor. Mr. Hall had tried to pour himself some water from a pitcher on a small table beside his bed, but his left arm — his only arm — is weak and he dropped the pitcher. When I went in to clean it up, he shouted at me to go away. He said he did not want anyone to see him as he was. I tried to tell him that I just wanted to mop up the water and pick up the pieces of broken jug, but he wouldn't hear of it. He shouted at me until I left the room and was not content until I had shut the door. I was shaking when I sat down again on the sofa. He was so pale and thin, and the right sleeve of his shirt hung empty. It was all I could do to not stare at it and to keep the pity from my eyes. But the poor man. How is he to manage now?

When Mrs. Hall returned I told her what had happened, and she rushed into his room. She stayed for a long time.

### December 8, 1847

The doctor came again today to see Mr. Hall. When he came out of the sick room, he and Mrs. Hall talked for a long time in hushed tones. Mrs. Hall was quiet for the rest of the day. She seemed lost in thought and worry.

### December 9, 1847

A quiet day. I amused Lucy as best I could while Mrs. Hall sat in a chair by the window. Her face was lined with worry. I hope Mr. Hall is not worse. She has not said anything about her conversation with the doctor yesterday.

## December 10, 1847

After Lucy lay down for her nap, Mrs. Hall called me to her. Mr. Hall's wounds are going to take a long time to mend, she said. His right leg is badly damaged, and without his right arm, it is unlikely that he will be able to walk without assistance. Continuing with the farm is not going to be possible. Her voice trembled as she told me that she has decided to write to her family back in England to tell them that it would be best if she and Mr. Hall returned there in the spring. Her father is in business and she is sure that he can find a position that is suitable for Mr. Hall that will not require much physical effort. She will also be able to rely on her own family for help, not only with Mr. Hall but with Lucy and the new baby as well.

I am ashamed to say that while she was telling me this, I was thinking only of myself. Was she going to ask me to go with her? I could not do that. I could never leave Michael. But what would become of me when she left? Would I be able to find another position? Would I ever find another employer as kind as Mrs. Hall?

"I would like to take you with me," Mrs. Hall said. "But I cannot. I'm sorry, Johanna. I know how hard things have been for you. You have been a part of this family. I know Lucy will miss you and so will I."

She also told me not to worry because this was all

a long way off. She promised to help me find another position in the area before she leaves, and to write me a good reference. I had tears in my eyes when I thanked her.

## *December 11, 1847*

Mr. Hall improves a little every day. Mrs. Hall says that he is cheerier now that Lucy is here. He reads to her every night before she goes to bed.

## *December 13, 1847*

Michael is found! What a glorious day! Here is what happened.

The morning was bright and sunny, and Lucy was restless in the house. More than once Mrs. Hall scolded her for not being quiet while her father slept. Finally I offered to take her for a walk through town. We had a jolly time making tracks in the snow and sliding on the ice of a pond. On the way home Lucy asked for a story and I told her one. I was nearly finished when the house came into sight and I saw Mrs. Hall standing in the door, clutching a shawl around her. She seemed to be watching for someone. My heart seemed to stop in my chest and I feared the worst. Mr. Hall must have taken a bad turn, and Mrs. Hall must be waiting for the doctor. Why else would she be standing there in the cold?

Then she caught sight of us and waved for us to

hurry. I didn't want to alarm Lucy, so I proposed a race. She ran ahead of me and her mother bundled her up into her arms. Mrs. Hall kissed her and smiled at me, which was a great relief. Clearly I was mistaken and all was well with Mr. Hall. Perhaps Mrs. Hall had just been eager to have Lucy back again. Perhaps her father had been asking for her.

Mrs. Hall continued to smile as she helped Lucy out of her boots and coat. I was about to go to the room I shared with Lucy at the back of the house when Mrs. Hall said, "You have a visitor, Johanna."

No wonder she was smiling. The Fentons had come to visit. Fanny was here! And all this time I had thought I might never see her again. I hurried into the parlour.

But it was not the Fentons.

It was Connor!

He stood when he saw me and looked me over and laughed, declaring that he would not have recognized me in such a fine dress and with meat on my bones for a change. I ran to him and hugged him. But how on earth had he found me?

As Connor told the story, he had lived for several weeks with the family who took in Daniel and who, he said, were taking good care of him — better than Connor himself could have done. Reassured but restless, he had gone back to Montreal to look for work.

"I was in the square near the house owned by the

nuns," he said. "Can you guess who I saw there?"

I stared at him, hardly daring to hope.

It was Michael! He had seen Michael. But he isn't in Montreal. He's living on a farm with Uncle Liam.

"Does he know about me?"

"He knows that you did not perish in the sheds," Connor said. Sister Marie-France's second letter had finally reached Uncle Liam. As soon as Michael realized I was NOT dead, he travelled to Montreal, hoping that the nuns would know where I was. But when he got there, he was disappointed. Sister Marie-France had died of the fever.

Tears sprang to my eyes when Connor told me this. The news of Michael had been like a bright summer sun. But this news of Sister Marie-France was like black clouds. Why did bad always follow good? Why couldn't everyone live happily ever after?

According to Connor, Sister Marie-France's replacement was not as organized as Sister Marie-France had been. She did not know what had become of me.

"Then how did you find me?" I asked.

He told me that Michael had left Montreal and gone back to Uncle Liam's farm. Connor stayed to find work, which was not easy. The economy was bad, there were so many people seeking employment, and there was widespread resentment against all the Irish who had flooded the city. Connor said he had been welcomed and fairly treated when he'd first arrived as an orphan, but soon found himself just one Irish lad among thousands who stood accused of stealing jobs from the people of Montreal and under-cutting their wages by agreeing to work for whatever an employer might offer. But Connor was lucky. He was hired on by the boss of a logging camp, although not the same one that had employed Mr. Hall. There he had met a boy, a cook's helper. The boy was Irish as well, so he and Connor became friendly. "He likes to say he's an honest man," Connor told me, "even though he got his start in this country as a thief. He says he knows you, Johanna, and that you do not approve of him. His name is Tommy Ryan."

I stared at Connor. I could hardly believe it. Tommy Ryan — that young thief I met in Montreal. He told Connor where I had gone. Connor said he immediately found someone who could write a letter for him to Michael. Then he set out to find me. It was the Fentons who told him I was in Sherbrooke.

Tears of joy ran down my cheeks. Michael was alive and well. Uncle Liam was well too. It was only then that I thought of Connor's brother Kerry, who had been taken off the ship at Grosse Isle. When I asked about him, Connor turned sombre. Kerry had died the day we departed by steamer to Montreal. Poor Connor. He, like me, had only one brother left in this world.

I looked at Mrs. Hall. My dream was coming true, while hers had been dashed. But her face brimmed with joy, and she hugged me and told me how happy she was that my brother was found. She gently explained that I would have to wait until spring for the St. Lawrence to reopen before I would be able to travel by boat, and said she knew how hard it would be to wait, but that meanwhile I would be such a great help to her.

It was then that I knew everything had worked out for the best. I would stay with her until we were both able to begin our travels — she to her family across the ocean and I to mine inland. I hugged her back and told her she was as close to my own mother as I could ever have hoped to find.

I am almost at the end of the book I brought from home. As soon as it is finished, I will use the new book Fanny gave me to record my new life when it begins.

# Epilogue

When at long last spring arrived, Johanna travelled by boat to Cobourg in what is now Ontario and then by wagon to Peterborough. Peterborough was named for Peter Robinson, who brought nearly two thousand Irish settlers there in 1825. Here Johanna was finally reunited with Michael, whom she hardly recognized, as he had grown taller and filled out, from being able to eat his fill. She met her Uncle Liam for the first time. He owned some land near the Otonabee River. He had built a small cabin and had started to clear the land of trees so that he could plant crops and graze some cows.

Johanna fit easily into the small household, happily filling the role of housekeeper, quickly putting to good use all the skills she had learned with Mrs. Hall and Mrs. Lyons, and adding new ones to her store of knowledge. As she reported to Fanny in the first of many letters over the years, her cooking rapidly improved. So did her knitting. Her scarves no longer turned out lopsided, and the thick socks she made kept her uncle's and brother's feet warm in winter. She found special pleasure in collecting scraps of fabric so that she could piece together quilts that drew on her memories. One of lush greens reminded her of her home in Ireland. Another, pure white with small bursts of colour, conjured up early spring growth emerging from the depths of winter. Riots of colour depicted patches of wildflowers deep in summer.

With Michael's help, Uncle Liam cleared his land and built a snug little farmhouse to replace the cabin he and Michael had been living in when Johanna arrived. It wasn't long before Michael fell in love with Mary Kehoe, the daughter of a neighbouring farmer. He married and brought her to live at Uncle Liam's farm. Mary and Johanna became fast friends and spent many an evening knitting and sewing, and talking and laughing.

Johanna became as expert at dressmaking as she was at quilting. She was soon sought out by other women to help with sewing chores or to make dresses for them and their daughters. It was while she was making a bridal dress for a miller's daughter that she met Thomas Macdonnell, the bride-to-be's brother. He was tall and handsome, with dark curly hair and clear blue eyes. But it was his easy laugh and the calm delight he took in life that drew Johanna. His good humour reminded her of her father, and he had a store of tales like her grandfather and a gift for bringing them alive as he told them. Johanna fell in love with him almost immediately and did not hesitate for even a moment when he proposed marriage.

Johanna and Thomas's first child, a son, was born before their first wedding anniversary. Johanna named him Francis Joseph for her father and for the patron saint of his occupation. A daughter soon followed. Johanna named her Eileen, after her mother. Three more children came, each little more than a year apart — Patrick, Connor and, finally, Anna, named for Johanna's childhood friend. Johanna was never able to trace her friend's whereabouts, but thought of her often in what soon would become called "the old days back home." She was grateful that all five children survived their younger years.

Johanna and Thomas regaled their children with stories. Johanna told them all about her family and the country from which they had come. She told them about the good years as well as the bad, about the journey across the ocean and the days of tremendous sorrow. She also told them the stories of Lusmore the humpback, the beautiful maiden, and all the other tales of banshees, fairies, pookas and leprechauns that she had learned from her grandfather. When her daughters were old enough, she let them read the cramped little record she had kept of her first months in Canada.

Johanna continued to write about the important events in her life, as well as many letters — to Mrs. Hall back in England with her family, and to Connor, who was not very good about writing back, but who came to visit once when Johanna's children were small, and again when her son got married.

Johanna always wore her father's St. Joseph medallion around her neck on a silver chain, even though it had been rubbed so smooth that it looked like a blank disc of tin. Whenever she thought about her parents, which she did often, her fingers went to the disc and she rubbed it and believed that she could still feel the warmth of her father's fingers upon it.

Johanna lived to be a very old woman and welcomed twenty-three grandchildren and fifteen great-grandchildren into the world. She made each one a small quilt, rich with the colours of Ireland, and when she took them on her knee, she told them tales of the old country in the soft Irish lilt that she never lost.

# Historical Note

"The Great Hunger" (*An Gorta Mór* in Irish) or the Irish Potato Famine of 1845–1851 was one of the most devastating events in Irish history. Before the famine struck, Ireland had a population of eight million. By the time it ended, nearly one million Irish had died of starvation and disease and another million had fled the country as emigrants. About three hundred thousand of these emigrants boarded ships for Canada.

Even before the famine struck, Ireland was a poor country. Most of the land in the countryside was owned by English landlords; most were Protestants who did not even live in Ireland. They rented out little parcels of land to Irish Catholic farmers. Many of these tenant farmers were so poor that they lived in one-room cabins and slept on straw on the ground. Poverty was made worse in Ireland by the rapid growth in population in the first four decades of the 1800s. The increasing number of people led to an increasing demand for land. Farmers began to cultivate land that was not suited for many crops. This land could, however, grow potatoes.

Potatoes are easy to grow, and have a high yield per plant. One acre of land could produce enough potatoes to feed an entire family for a year. Potatoes are rich in protein, carbohydrates and vitamins. As improbable as it sounds, it is possible to stay healthy by eating just potatoes. In fact, it was said that the peasants in Ireland were healthier than their counterparts in England who ate bread as their main food. Bread is not as nutritious as potatoes.

By the time of the famine, over one-third of the population of Ireland lived almost exclusively on potatoes. Adult males might eat an astonishing 5 to 6 kilograms of boiled potatoes per day, while women and children consumed less. When possible, milk, butter, cabbage or fish were mixed with the potatoes, and added flavour and nutrition. In this way, the Irish were able to support themselves — until disaster struck.

In the fall of 1845, the potato crop throughout Europe failed. Just before harvest, the leaves on many potato plants turned black and rotted. When the potatoes were dug up, they looked fine. But within a day or two they had rotted into a slimy mush that gave off a horrible smell. No one knew it at the time, but the potato crop had been attacked by a fungus that spread easily in the air. The effect of the potato blight was especially hard in Ireland, where so many people relied on potatoes as their main source of food.

Today if such a disaster struck, relief organizations would swing into action and do everything they could to help the starving. But this was not the case in the

1840s. There were no organizations able to offer large-scale relief.

By the spring of 1846 the British government, which controlled Ireland, took some steps to help the famine victims. It set up programs to pay Irish farmers in return for public works, such as building roads. But this was badly organized and the money the workers were paid was often not nearly enough to feed a whole family. Also, some of the workers were already too weak from hunger to be able to work. Some even died from starvation and overexertion.

The British government also bought corn from America to sell to the starving, but many of the Irish could not afford to buy it. American corn, called "Indian corn" or "maize," was unknown in Ireland. Those who could afford it did not know how to cook it properly, and suffered from stomach ailments and diarrhea as a result.

By the second year of the famine there had been a change in government in England. The new government stopped all food relief to Ireland. It hoped that the new crop of potatoes would be healthy and said that it did not want the Irish to become dependent on handouts from England.

But the potato crop in 1846 was not healthy. The famine got worse. People ate whatever they could find — seaweed, roots, weeds, even grass. They sold whatever they could in order to pay their rent to their landlords, so that they would not be homeless as well as hungry. On top of that, the winter of 1846–1847 was one of the harshest in Irish history. People froze as well as starved. Many became sick. The immediate cause of death for many of those who died during the famine was not starvation but, rather, diseases such cholera, typhus, dysentery and famine dropsy that preyed on their weakened bodies. So great was the death toll that people were often buried without coffins or were dumped into mass graves. There were even stories of coffins being built with trap doors in the bottom so that they could be used over and over.

Starving, with nothing to eat and no money to pay their rent, hundreds of thousands of Irish men, women and children were turned out of their homes. This suited many landlords who were eager to increase their incomes by growing wheat or raising cattle and sheep, which they could not do as long as they had tenant farmers occupying their land. They evicted tenants who owed back rent and pulled down their little houses so that they could never return. They also began to pay to send these now landless farmers overseas. Those who were sent or chose to go to Canada were transported in cargo ships — usually ships that had brought timber to England — that installed wooden berths and crammed in as many passengers as they could, so they could make as much money as possible returning to North America.

Because disease and death were so common aboard these vessels, they came to be called "coffin ships."

The trip from Liverpool (or from ports in Ireland itself) to Quebec was 4800 kilometres and, depending on the wind and the weather, could take from five or six weeks to three months. Passage included some food, but often not enough to keep a person healthy. Drinking water often went bad before the end of the journey. The accommodations were terrible: people were crowded together below deck, with no ventilation, no sanitary facilities, and no shortage of disease-carrying rats. They shared their space with those who fell ill or were already sick when they boarded the ship. In these conditions, disease spread quickly and easily.

Passengers who survived the journey were inspected by a doctor when they arrived in Quebec. Those who were ill were quarantined on Grosse-Île, a small island about 48 kilometres from Quebec City. In 1847 so many ships arrived with so many ill passengers that Grosse-Île, overcrowded and short of doctors and nurses, was a place where patients were almost certain to die. The medical authorities were so overwhelmed that many passengers did not even receive a proper medical inspection. They were sent by steamer to Montreal, Kingston and Toronto, where they often arrived sick and dying. These cities tried to provide medical treatment, but it was often too little too late.

It is hard to know how many Irish died in the famine in Ireland, how many emigrated, and how many survived the journey. Record-keeping was poor, passengers were not required to register their place of birth, and many ship captains did not keep proper passenger lists. But some historians estimate that about one hundred thousand Irish made the journey to Canada in 1847, and that one in five of these died from disease and malnutrition. Many children arrived in Canada as orphans. These children were generally well cared for by religious and charitable organizations, and many were adopted by Quebec families. Most people arrived with nothing and had to work hard to find employment.

By the mid-1850s, ten thousand Irish called Quebec City their home, and many more had settled in Montreal and found employment as shopkeepers, artisans, tailors, shoemakers and policemen. The majority of Montreal Irish, however, worked as labourers, servants, coachmen, blacksmiths and carpenters, and lived in Griffintown, where factories stood beside the Lachine Canal. Griffintown was widely described as a slum.

In Toronto at the same time, one quarter of the fifty thousand inhabitants were Irish, the largest national group in the city. Most lived near the lakefront in Cabbagetown, so called because of the cabbage patches the Irish grew in their yards.

Irish immigrants settled in many other places in Canada, such as Ontario's Ottawa Valley, Kingston and area, and Peterborough. Hundreds of thousands more settled in the United States, in places like Boston, New York, Baltimore and Philadelphia, and founded Irish-Catholic communities that remain a part of the identity of those cities today.

*Irish children dig what potatoes they can salvage out of the ground. The potato blight rotted most of the potatoes before they could be harvested.*

*A destitute father and child stand near their stone cottage. The famine forced tens of thousands of "Poor Irish" off the land when the crop failed and they could not afford to pay rent to their landlords.*

EMIGRANTS ARRIVAL AT CORK.—A SCENE ON THE QUAY.

*Emigrants huddle with their meagre belongings at dockside in Cork, before embarking on ships that will take them across the Atlantic to North America.*

*Hundreds of thousands of emigrants crossed the ocean in hopes of finding a better life in Canada. They endured voyages of up to six or even twelve weeks, much of it spent crammed below decks, where illness such as typhus and cholera spread easily in the crowded conditions.*

*Ships wait in the St. Lawrence near Grosse-Île (about 48 km from Quebec City) to offload ill passengers. Their families often had to remain in quarantine, or continue the voyage without them.*

*Those quarantined in the Grosse-Île fever sheds lived in squalid conditions, despite the efforts of the staff trying to care for them. Many who entered the sheds never emerged, except to be buried.*

*This cooking stove from 1862 shows a hot water tank and an oven for roasting — major improvements to cooking over direct flame in a suspended kettle.*

*Candle-making had been a long process of dipping string into melted tallow and allowing it to dry in stages. Molds such as this one made the work simpler.*

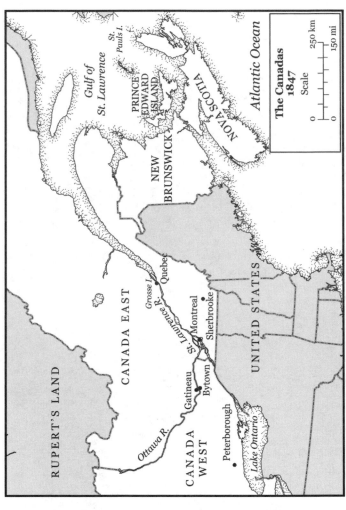

*Eastern Canada in 1847. Famine Irish landed in eastern ports, with many moving further inland to Quebec, Montreal, Kingston and the Ottawa Valley in Canada, as well as Baltimore, New York, Philadelphia and Boston in the United States.*

# Acknowledgements

Cover cameo (detail): Christen Brun, *A Basket of Ribbons*, Image thanks to the Art Renewal Center ® www.artrenewal.org.

Cover background (detail) and page 159: *Emigrants Arrival at Cork — The Scene on the Quay,* Library and Archives Canada, C-003904.

Page 157: *The Irish Potato Famine*, Illustrated London News Ltd / Mary Evans Picture Library.

Page 158: *A destitute father and child in Mienies, Ireland*; Illustrated London News Ltd / Mary Evans Picture Library.

Page 160: *Thousands of people came from Europe,* from *Historical Etchings/Travel*, Crabtree Publishing Company, p. 4.

Page 161: *Boats waiting in line on the St. Lawrence River, to be welcomed on Grosse Île,* courtesy of Bernard Duchesne/Collections Parcs Canada.

Page 162: *Early quarantine station facilities at Grosse Île,* 1832, courtesy of Bernard Duchesne/Collections Parcs Canada.

Page 163 (upper): *Cook stove,* C.W. Jefferys / Library and Archives Canada, Acc. No. 1972-26-825.

Page 163 (lower): *Candle mold,* Image courtesy of the Niagara Historical Society & Museum, 969.32.

Page 164: Map by Paul Heersink/Paperglyphs.

The publisher wishes to thank Barbara Hehner for her attention to the factual details, and Dr. Ross Fair, Ryerson University, for sharing his historical expertise.

*To Mary Ellen Carson McClintock*

# About the Author

"I have always been interested in history and how ordinary people managed through all the wars, plagues, famines, natural disasters and other hardships of life throughout the ages," says Norah McClintock. "My mother has a somewhat more personal interest in history — she has spent many years researching her genealogy to try to understand the lives of those who preceded her.

"Tracing one's family tree is not as easy as it might sound to anyone who was raised in the age of computers, when it seems that there is almost too much personal information available. We have records galore these days, and the challenge is protecting them and safeguarding people's privacy. But go back a generation or two, and things are entirely different. Records were kept on paper, which could burn (along with the buildings where they were stored) or succumb to floods, or neglect — or simply be discarded or lost. And that's assuming records existed at all. In many cases they didn't.

"It is very difficult to say with certainty exactly how many people died in Ireland during the famine, how many emigrated to other countries in the famine years, how many died on the voyage itself or immediately afterward, or exactly where the survivors ended up. My great-great-grandmother is a case in point.

"I know, thanks to my mother's research, that her name was Mary Ellen O'Leary. I know that she left Ireland during the famine. I know that she died sometime after she left. I know that she had at least three children. But after that, there are more questions than answers.

"Was she really from Tipperary, as my great-grandmother told my mother? In which year did she leave Ireland? Did she die on the voyage, or on Grosse-Île, or later, when she reached Pembroke, Ontario? I don't know. Two of her children were named Mary and Edward, and they were born in Ireland. There is another child, possibly named James. On the 1861 census, he is reported as having been born in Canada. What does that tell me about my grandmother, assuming it's true?"

\* \* \*

Norah McClintock is best known as one of Canada's top mystery writers for young adults. Some of her most popular series are Chloe and Levesque, Mike and Riel and Robyn Hunter, each featuring a teenage sleuth. She is a five-time winner of the Arthur Ellis Award for crime fiction, for *Mistaken Identity, The Body in the Basement, Sins of the Father, Scared to Death* and *Break and Enter*. She was also nominated for the Arthur Ellis Award for her non-fiction title, *Body, Crime, Suspect,* and for the prestigious Anthony Award for *No Escape.*

Though McClintock's degree is in History and she has worked as a volunteer at Toronto's Spadina House, this is her first historical novel. As she says, "It's time to put that knowledge to use."

**Library and Archives Canada Cataloguing in Publication**

McClintock, Norah
A sea of sorrows : the typhus epidemic diary of Johanna
Leary / Norah McClintock.

(Dear Canada)
ISBN 978-1-4431-0710-5

1. Irish--Canada--History--Juvenile fiction. I. Title.
II. Series: Dear Canada

PS8575.C62S43 2012      jC813'.54      C2012-901655-1

6  5  4  3  2  1      Printed in Canada  114      12  13  14  15  16

The text was set in Minion.

First printing September 2012

MIX
From responsible
sources
FSC® C016245

*Alone in an Untamed Land,* The Filles du Roi *Diary of Hélène St. Onge* by Maxine Trottier

*Banished from Our Home,* The Acadian Diary *of Angélique Richard* by Sharon Stewart

*Blood Upon Our Land,* The North West Resistance Diary *of Josephine Bouvier* by Maxine Trottier

*Brothers Far from Home,* The World War I Diary *of Eliza Bates* by Jean Little

*A Christmas to Remember,* Tales of Comfort and Joy

*Days of Toil and Tears,* The Child Labour Diary *of Flora Rutherford* by Sarah Ellis

*The Death of My Country,* The Plains of Abraham Diary *of Geneviève Aubuchon* by Maxine Trottier

*A Desperate Road to Freedom,* The Underground Railroad Diary *of Julia May Jackson* by Karleen Bradford

*Exiles from the War,* The War Guests Diary *of Charlotte Mary Twiss* by Jean Little

*Footsteps in the Snow,* The Red River Diary *of Isobel Scott* by Carol Matas

Go to www.scholastic.ca/dearcanada for information on the
Dear Canada series — see inside the books, read an excerpt
or a review, post a review, and more.